# KINGDOM
## OF
## GODS
## AND
## RUIN

### CAROLINE PECKHAM
### SUSANNE VALENTI

*This novella is set 1000 years before the events of A Game of Malice and Greed.*
*Before the Fae fell.*
*Before the gods abandoned the world.*
*Welcome to Osaria...*

*A thousand years ago the Fae fell from the grace of the gods with a single lie. In that moment, a prophecy was spoken into the world with their only hope cast upon its wings.*

*A glint of gold waiting in the gloom,*
*A deadly garden, a sunken tomb.*
*When a soldier glimpses beyond the veil,*
*And a thief is tempted by a forgotten trail.*

*A man of sin, and man of steel,*
*Shall form a fragile, fate-bound deal.*
*But temptation may lead men astray,*
*While Herdat stirs among the Fallen Fae.*

*Her dark servant shall gain eternal power,*
*If the dead man wakes within the final hour.*
*For the Prophet lingers in the deep,*
*Waiting for his chance to reap.*

*A vessel soaked in ink and blood,*
*Shall face the hands of hungry gods.*
*But all fates do not lie with men,*
*For there is a power far greater than them.*

*A princess with an arrow sharp as diamond flies,*
*While a city watches as a beast of fury dies.*
*And a Fae who never fell will shine,*
*With a magic older than the dawn of time.*

*All fates will twist and coil as one,*
*Before the curse shall be undone.*
*And a warrior born of sin shall rise,*
*When the shell gleams, and they punish our lies.*

# CHAPTER ONE

Cracks tore through the white walls of the temple, the world itself screaming as the home of the sun god, Saresh, was ripped asunder. Ancient paintings on the walls split down the middle, depictions of Saresh offering out the gift of life to the first of the Fae were blasted apart as the wrathful fury of the deities made the air quake.

The ground beneath my bare feet bucked and quaked until I was thrown onto my back so violently that pain lanced through my flesh, and my long, ebony hair was thrown across my golden eyes.

The thin, white nightgown I wore tangled around my legs as I scrambled backwards, trying to avoid the statues which toppled and smashed on the marble floor, the face of Saresh shattering a thousand times over as if he wanted all traces of his history destroyed.

The intricate marks of the gods blazed on what remained of the walls, filled with golden light as their rage made the world tremble.

*"We gave you everything,"* the air itself seemed to cry. *"And all we asked of you was virtue. All we begged for was truth."*

Beneath me, a crack ripped through the marble floor, and I rolled over, tearing at the nightgown as I fought to get up, throwing myself aside to avoid the lumps of masonry falling from the domed, golden roof of the temple.

There had been other Fae here worshipping with me. Those who had come to pay homage to Saresh at the midday rite. But they had vanished as surely as the peace had been broken. One moment sitting all around me, the next, banished as if they had never been here at all.

What had I done to deserve this?

*"You know the black deeds of your heart!"* the world screamed, and I screamed with it, a lump of glimmering golden tile crashing down from the

roof and slicing into my shoulder.

"I didn't mean to," I gasped as I lurched aside, blood pulsing through my fingers as I clamped them over the wound, my gaze on the distant door and the sunlight beyond. If I could only reach it, then I might stand a chance.

But the light was fading, the golden glow sinking into grey, then black, nothing but shattered starlight peering back at me as I ran for the arched doorway. It only seemed to grow more distant, no matter how fast I moved, and a sob tore from my throat as I saw the way my fate was falling.

"Please," I begged of the gods who had cursed me. "Please, understand why I-"

*"There will be no mercy,"* they spat, many voices as one. *"There is only the end."*

Power slammed into me with such violence that the air was torn from my lungs. I crumpled, my knees splitting open on the stone floor. My power was dragged from me, all that had made me what I was ripped free and returned to those who had bestowed it upon me. My Affinities were cleaved from my veins, the magical connection they had built between me and the world snapping like the chords of a harp sliced with a razor, the off-tune melody they released like a cry of death as my gifts were lost.

A sob caught in my throat as I tried to reach for those parts of my soul, the power which had lived in my veins for years upon years spilling from me like grains of sand through my fingers, impossible to hold on to.

The gods were taking away all they had ever offered us. Our magic, our Affinities, our immortality. I could feel it racing out of me as I shook beneath the force of its removal. I was consumed by the fear of what I would become now, and I begged the gods for a mercy which they had no inclination to give.

The ground broke apart beneath me and I gasped, my stomach swooping as I fell with another scream tearing from my throat.

But it wasn't my end I feared as the fires of the pit yawned wide for my rotten soul. It was the end of all as we knew it which sent me careering into the dark, our demise spiralling ever closer, and the wrath of the gods insurmountable in its violence.

## CHAPTER TWO

I was hurled from the nightmare of prophecy and fell panting and heaving within sweat-soaked sheets.

"What is it?" a rough voice groaned from the darkness.

I flinched as my mind spun with the dream and I found myself back in my bed once more, the air still around us, the balmy breeze sweeping in through the gossamer curtains.

"I…" My heart was thrashing so violently that I could barely form the words, true tears wet on my cheeks, the dream having felt so real that I was struggling to take in my surroundings.

There was the metal framework at the foot of my bed, the sheets twisted around my legs, and the space beyond it where the curtains moved in that familiar pattern before the open doors to my balcony. The candle on the mantle above the unlit fire had long since burned out, but I could see it there, the nub and melted wax coating the bronze holder.

I looked to the wooden armoire and let my gaze trail over the whirls in the design above the doors, counting them slowly as my thrashing heart began to settle, and I gave in to the feeling of safety and familiarity which filled this place.

The heated air rolling in from the distant desert was as familiar to me as my own breath, the sounds of the blue-feathered harocs calling to one another in the trees outside letting me know that the night was still at its fullest.

Calvari rolled closer to me, the sheets shifting and the pale moonlight gilding the bare skin of his broad back as he pushed himself onto his elbows to look down at me.

I blinked up at him, his long hair falling forward over his shoulders as the face I had once known so well pinched with concern.

Reality returned to me as I remembered the tavern last night, the singing and the Faery wine. Calvari's unit had returned from the Banished Lands, another battle won and more lives lost. But he'd returned among the rest of the Fated Legion, a few new battle scars marking the dark skin of his powerful body. And just like we had many times before, we'd fallen prey to the sinful nature of my secondary Affinity for seduction, gifted to me by the god Bentos, and I'd brought him back to my bed.

"You had a nightmare?" he asked slowly, his weight shifting on the bed as he reached out to brush a tangled strand of my ebony hair away from my eyes.

"It felt so real," I murmured, distracted by the lingering fear of the nightmare.

"Did it hold a taste of prophecy?" Calvari asked seriously, and I frowned as I noted the metallic taste on my tongue which the Fae had always known to associate with the gods.

"Maybe," I hedged, the horror of what I'd witnessed too awful to be a true rendering of the future. "A warning, perhaps. The world was falling down around me, the gods were filled with wrath. They stripped me of my power…I…"

"It sounds like they had reason to be angry with you. Have you been up to no good while I've been off fighting the Banished?" Calvari's lips curled up at the corner, and I narrowed my eyes at him, the fear from the dream fading as I settled back into reality once more.

There were no cracks in the walls, no angry gods screaming at me, and my power still imbued my limbs. Though my most prominent Affinity was for healing, here, alone with him, I was far more caught up in the talents Bentos had given me.

"When am I ever bad enough to incite the gods?" I taunted, and his smile grew.

He wasn't the most handsome of Fae, but there had always been something about that smile which drew me to him. It didn't hurt that his training with the Fated Warriors had moulded his body into a work of art worth studying for hours on end, and I liked that he didn't ever flinch from the sharpness of my tongue.

We were what we were. Two Fae who enjoyed sharing our bodies. Easy, simple, no promises holding us to anything, no vows or declarations hanging in the air between us. When he returned from war bloody, broken, and haunted by the things he'd seen and experienced, I gave him a distraction, a release, simplicity. While he gave me…

"Bad is what you're best at, Kyra," Calvari purred, his hand shifting to my thigh beneath the thin sheet as our thoughts wandered to the truth of that fact.

I bit down on my bottom lip and my gaze drifted down his chest, the long scar which stood out across his abs letting me know how close he had come to death this time.

"The Legion is smaller than it was when you last set out," I said, my hand finding the edge of that scar and my healing Affinity making my fingertips

12

tingle as I inspected it. "You lost a lot of warriors in the last four years."

"We did," Calvari grunted, his gaze dimming with that reality, and for a moment I could hear the screams of the dying, scent the blood on the air, feel the hopelessness of war surrounding us. "The Banished hatched three dragon eggs. They caught us off guard more than once."

He tugged on my knee to widen my legs, and I obliged him as his fingers shifted higher, seeking the wet heat of my core, the oblivion we could claim in this bed.

I wasn't running from the kinds of horrors he had lived through, but I was always seeking my own kind of escape with him too. Escape from this stagnation I felt in my life. This eternal nothing where days spilled into weeks and months and years and I just…was.

I didn't know when I had first begun to feel like my destiny wasn't in this empire, or when I had realised that I would never find true peace here, but I felt like a bird in a cage within this city.

I yearned for adventure, a different reality, something *more*. I just didn't know how to begin seeking it.

"Surely the dragons didn't serve them willingly?" I asked, my eyes meeting Calvari's as he sank two fingers into me and coaxed a moan from my lips.

"They were chained," he admitted, watching me as I writhed beneath him, drinking in the sight of me at his mercy. "Beaten, scarred. It was a terrible crime to witness. We released two into death before my unit drew back."

"And the third?" I asked, my heart aching for that most sacred of creatures, even as my mind began to scatter beneath the feeling of his fingers deep inside me.

"They still have it," he admitted, the words sending a crack of sadness through my heart. "We plan on seeking out Azurea and asking her to fly into battle with us when we return to the front," Calvari added, his mouth moving to my throat as his thumb found my clit and he began working me harder. "Perhaps we can convince a dragon to fly into war like they did in the days of old."

My spine arched against the sheets as a cry of pleasure fell from my lips, and I imagined the fear such a thing might inspire in the Banished. A fully grown dragon flying into war above the Fated Legion. No doubt they'd die from terror alone.

"Nothing could stand between you and victory then," I panted, and Calvari chuckled darkly, the sound a sin against my skin.

"Nothing will stand between me and victory now," he swore, his cock driving against my thigh as he fucked me with his hand, and I drew closer to the edge.

I almost came for him, a good girl bending to his masterful fingers, but I knew we both wanted to work harder for it than that.

I turned my head to capture his lips, the thin line of a scar pressing against the softness of my mouth as I tasted him, the bite of stubble raking against my chin.

He was a brute of a man, built for war and ruin, his Affinities all linked to fighting and battle. But my Affinity for the pleasures of the flesh was more than a match for his unerring strength.

I pushed him back suddenly, pressing his spine to the mattress as I swung my thigh over his body and knocked his fingers from me.

I bit down on his lip and kissed him harder, the fear of my nightmare fading as the power of my gifts rose and my skin sang with need.

I broke our kiss, reaching for the curved metal of the headboard as I moved up his body and knelt over his face.

Calvari obliged me, his mouth locking over my clit as his large hands moved to grip my arse and he dragged me down to sit on his face.

I moaned as he sank his tongue into me, rocking my hips and beginning to ride his mouth, sighing loudly every time his tongue circled just right.

My right hand locked tight around the metal of the headboard and I began to tease my nipple with my left, my breasts full and heavy, bouncing softly as I rode his face and the need in me heightened.

I was insatiable when this power was awakened in me. My body filled with a hunger that I could never fully satisfy, but Calvari had the stamina it took to at least take the edge off my need.

He devoured me with all the unsated lust he had gathered in the years he'd spent at war. He'd told me once that he never took lovers while he was deployed, though he had never asked me to withhold in turn, he simply preferred to lean into his Affinities while at war. He was a warrior honed for death and bloodshed, and the power the gods had gifted him made him a perfect weapon for such things. When he was in the battle camps, he became simply that; a machine intended for destruction. Passion and needs of the flesh went unanswered until he returned to us here in the homelands, where it was safe and he could let his guard down without risking his survival.

It made sense. And it also made for an utterly ravenous partner in the bedroom when he returned.

I came with a cry of ecstasy, my body bowing forward as I leaned on the headboard for support.

Calvari lifted me so he could get to his knees at my back, and he was inside me before I could even catch my breath, the feeling of his cock sinking deep and striking hard enough to push out all lingering fear from that nightmare.

His hand fisted my hair, his teeth nipping at the soft skin of my throat as he tugged my head back to give himself the room he desired, and I hooked an arm back around his neck to hold myself there.

My other hand dropped to my clit, and I rode my fingers in time with every savage thrust of his cock inside me, moaning loudly with each pump of his hips.

Calvari gripped my waist as he fucked me harder, stealing a brutal kiss from my lips before pushing me face down onto the bed and sinking in even deeper than before.

My hand was crushed between my body and the mattress, my fingers rutting against my clit in time with the punishing thrusts of his hips, and I called out for him to go harder, deeper, seeking oblivion in the release of this passion.

I felt his cock stiffening as he drew closer to his climax, mine just out of reach as I panted and writhed beneath him, and I pushed my hips up, demanding more from him with gasping pleas.

He gripped my arse as he pumped into me harder, faster, cursing my name as he tried to hold off his own release while chasing mine, and I rode my fingers more frantically, sweat rolling down my spine between us.

I swore as I finally found my outlet, biting down on the bedsheets as my pussy clamped tight around his cock and bliss trilled through my limbs. Calvari jerked out of me, groaning loudly as he came all over my arse, the hot splash of his cum against my skin bringing a breath of laughter to my lips.

"You're fucking ravenous as always, Kyra," he growled as he grabbed the sheet which had been covering us while we slept and used it to clean the evidence of his desire from my body.

"I'm ready to go again when you are," I teased as I rolled over to look at him, and he dropped back against the sheets with his chest heaving from exertion, a faint smile on his lips that told me he wanted to do that just as soon as he recovered.

We fucked and swapped stories of the years since we'd last seen one another then fucked again. The rhythm was endless, my need limitless as always, my body bringing his to ruin time and again, while his took the edge off of my lust as he made me come for him. Slowly, the night passed to dawn, and we finally fell into a heap of limbs and succumbed to sleep once more.

Or at least we did until the call of my sister's voice drew me from my bed, an amused curse passing my lips as I was dragged from slumber.

I left Calvari where he was, satisfied and a little lighter than he had been after a night lost in the feeling of our bodies against one another, the memories of war farther behind him once more.

There was a thin satin gown hanging by the door to my bathing chamber, and I pulled it on to cover my nakedness, the deep red colour contrasting prettily against the warm brown of my skin.

It was summer, and even an hour past dawn, the heat was stifling, the air thick and humidity rolling in from the river which carved through the centre of the city.

"Two more minutes or we'll come in and drag you from your bed with our bare hands!" Aalia called, amusement to her tone which let me know the twins were close by.

I ignored the door and headed for the window instead, stepping out onto the balcony and raising a hand to shield my eyes from the brightness of the morning light.

The lush green gardens beyond my room in the manor house I shared with my sister and her family were full of the chittering of small birds and rodents, the burbling of the stream at the foot of the hill a welcome I had received almost every day of my life.

My sister's husband, Aren, stood beneath the broad willow, his back to the bark as he eyed me with amusement, inclining his head towards the lower floor of the house just enough to confirm that Aalia and the twins were inside.

My lips quirked up at the corner, and I took several running steps before hopping up onto the low white wall which ringed my balcony.

I threw my arms out wide on either side of me and closed my eyes as I let myself topple from the edge.

My stomach swooped and my ebony hair whipped back, but before I could so much as drop a full foot, glimmering golden wings expanded from my spine, fluttering hard to catch my weight while the sun shone through their near-transparent membrane and made the world glitter around me.

I swept into the trees in utter silence, my skin tingling as my lesser Affinities for stealth and secrecy gifted from the god of tricksters, Carioth, helped me land silently, my bare feet pressing into the soft grass before my wings faded from existence again. The Affinities the gods gifted each of us upon our birth varied from Fae to Fae, most of us claiming a single dominant Affinity which supposedly matched the essence of our souls to perfection.

Mine was healing, a trait from the goddess Luciet, who had blessed me with a natural inclination towards medicine. It was magic, but it was also an ability, a part of who we were. I could sense illness, my instincts always helping me choose the correct remedies and treatments, while my innate magic made my own ability to heal near boundless. I could share that power with others to an extent when I willed it, but the magic which dwelled within me made my own body heal from practically any injury almost instantly.

In my youth, I'd wanted to use that gift to join the warriors fighting in the Banished Lands. I'd wanted to learn to fight and travel the world, my ability to heal from all wounds surely a gift any warrior would make great use of.

But our parents had squashed that dream quickly enough, along with the entire kingdom, I supposed. No woman could join the Legions, and only those Fae blessed with Affinities from Efries himself, the god of war and might, were allowed to go into battle. Perhaps I could have travelled to the outer reaches of the war camps to offer medical assistance, but it wasn't the same, and our parents had been no more likely to allow that even if I had tried to argue for it.

So here I'd stayed. For almost two hundred years, I'd woken up in this house, wandered the gardens, enjoyed the company of my sister and... well, not a lot of anything else, if I was being totally honest with myself.

Our parents had left to travel the western coast almost thirty years ago, visiting the various courts and sending occasional letters to their forgotten daughters. They hadn't even returned when Aalia had given birth to the twins. Twins! They were a miracle to be celebrated endlessly for our kind, especially with how rare it was for Fae to conceive at all. A child was a blessing, but twins were a gift from the gods themselves. Yet in the five years since their birth, the only thing our parents had sent was a note of congratulations, mixed in with commands for the way they expected the manor to be managed in their absence.

I supposed I might have been bitter if it weren't for the fact that we were all so much happier without them here. We were free to do as we wished, and I didn't have to suffer the endless judgements over how I spent my days and who I spent them with. There was no pressure to marry or to attend court more often – which I did as infrequently as possible. I was simply free, and if that came at the cost of a little restlessness and boredom, then I'd take the trade gladly.

Aren watched in amusement as I dropped to my hands and knees, his brown hair curling to his nape and the white shirt he wore loose around his neck in anticipation of the day's heat.

"Kiki!" a little voice shrieked, and I recognised my nephew, Rayan, as he tore around hunting for me.

I began to crawl through the long grass in his direction, grinning at the game as I closed in on him, growling like a desert beast to let him know I was on his trail.

Rayan shrieked and started running for the house, but before I could take chase, a little monster leapt from the grass to my right and landed on my back with a cry of victory.

I laughed as I rolled beneath Lina, her gleaming silver hair tumbling into her eyes as she fought to tickle me, and I made a good show of screaming and crying out for mercy.

Rayan leapt into the dogpile too, the little beast punching me in the side as he got too caught up in the game, and I quickly snatched his fist into my grip before pretending to gnaw on his arm.

He half howled, half fell apart with laughter and suddenly, Lina shifted sides, helping me tickle her brother as he kicked and shrieked between his laughs.

"Ah, Kyra, I should have known we'd find you rolling in the mud," Aalia teased.

Her shadow fell over us, and I released the two hellions as I rolled over to look up at my sister.

The golden light of dawn gilded her curling brunette hair in a crown of its own design, her skin lustrous in the light and her smile captivating. All over the kingdom, people whispered my sister's name and coveted her beauty. She was radiance embodied, this ethereal-looking creature who stole the breath from men and women alike when they laid their eyes upon her.

Some claimed Helios, the god of beauty and purity, had gifted her a drop of his own blood during her creation along with her Affinities, but I knew that the full truth of her beauty lay within her heart.

I was often compared to her, called the budding rose to her full bloom, and though it may have been meant as an insult, I had only ever seen that as a good thing. Alone, I was often called beautiful by those aiming to find their way into my bed. I was coveted and pursued enough not to concern myself with anything so petty as jealousy. My features had more of an edge to them than Aalia's, my eyes more feline, my smile sharper, and that suited me perfectly because we were not the same creature at our cores.

Aalia *was* beauty. She was kindness and compassion to the point of innocence, which frightened me sometimes. She saw the good in people and turned a blind eye to the bad all too often. I was a darker soul, and I knew it. I saw the bad in most before looking for the good, and I had more than a little of my own bad too. It made me somewhat jaded, but I liked to think I was more prepared for the reality of our world and therefore able to help shield my sister from the worst of it.

I had been more than thrilled when Aren had been the Fae to finally capture her interest fully. Marrying him in secret had been the one and only time I'd known her to defy our parents. They had hoped to capture a royal with her face, but Aalia had given her heart to a Fae whose dominant Affinity was for baking, thanks to Aliot, god of sustenance and health. Aren was a masterful baker, and I certainly had no complaints about the pastries I consumed endlessly, nor the biscuits I devoured with my tea.

No doubt that snub was the reason our parents hadn't returned to meet the twins, but that was their loss, so far as I was concerned, and the longer they stayed gone, the better.

"Is breakfast ready?" I asked, my gaze snapping to Aren who still lounged beneath his tree, hiding from the sun as always. I'd never known another Fae to be quite so scornful of the celestial being. He wasn't the kind to voice complaints, but I knew he far preferred it once the sun went down and the stars were shining upon his skin.

"Sadly, you missed it," he replied, and my mouth fell open in outrage.

"It's barely past dawn," I complained, getting to my feet as my stomach growled to voice its own complaints.

"Well, the twins wanted to see the sun rise, so we made a picnic of it on the roof." Aren shrugged innocently while the twins broke into tales of how beautiful it had been. Of how the sky had first turned from ebony to sapphire, then palest blue with streaks of orange and pink lighting the few clouds until they were burned up into nothing and the sun was reigning over the land in its entirety once more.

"There were some rather alarming sounds coming from your room," Aalia noted casually, her eyes flicking up towards my balcony doors which were flung wide as always.

"Were there now?" I asked, phrasing my reply as a question while she tried to back me into an admission. We couldn't tell a lie, one of the conditions the gods placed upon us during our creation, but that simply meant all Fae learned the art of evading answers from a young age.

"The children were quite curious," Aren added, shaking his head. "I told them that the warriors had returned from the Banished Lands."

"And that was answer enough for them?" I asked, looking to the children who had fallen into an all-out brawl.

I reached down to snatch Rayan off of his sister and tossed him over my shoulder where he started kicking and squealing in protest at being carried like a sack of potatoes.

"There was a convenient burst of drake fire towards the western mountains which drew their attention away," Aalia admitted. "So is that Calvari up there or…"

"I ran into him in the tavern last night," I admitted, and she grinned, making me roll my eyes. "You know it isn't like that between me and him. Don't go thinking you've found yourself a brother-in-law or anything ridiculous."

Aalia sighed dramatically before grabbing Lina and tossing her over her shoulder too, Aren falling into step with us as we headed into the house.

The scent of lotus blooms greeted me in the open space, and I inhaled deeply, looking at the arrangements Aalia had put together so skilfully. Beauty and purity. Her Affinities were seen as somewhat useless and merely decorative to many, but our family line held powerful magic, and the weight of hers shone through in everything that surrounded her. She could see beauty in almost everything. And she could see that which was truly ugly too – though she avoided such things as much as she could.

We set the twins free and they tore away from us, charging towards the table laid out with paints and parchment, both of them loudly claiming they would paint me the best portrait of the sunrise they'd seen.

Aren slipped his arm around Aalia's waist, tugging her close and murmuring something no doubt sickeningly sweet into her ear which drew a giggle from her lips before he stole a kiss from them.

She melted into him like she always did, and I smiled as I looked between the couple, their love for one another so potent I could practically taste it in the air.

"We've been summoned to court," Aren said as I moved to take a seat, and I fell still, glancing to my sister, then back to her husband.

"We?" I questioned, unease rising in my chest.

"The Fae of age who reside within our household," he clarified, waving a hand towards a letter which lay open on the table.

"It's just one evening," Aalia said softly, her attention shifting to the twins as they began work on their masterpieces.

"One too many," I muttered, scooping up the letter and examining it, hoping for some loophole to the royal summons.

"We can't be certain the emperor has any further interest in Aalia," Aren said, squeezing her hand in a way that was meant to be reassuring but only gave away his concern.

The last few times we'd visited Emperor Farish's court, he had paid my sister all too much attention. He'd even asked for a night with her, sending one of his guards to offer up the invitation as if it were some great honour to serve him in his bedroom. No matter that she was in love, married, a mother. Why should he care about such things?

The twins had been so young then that we had managed to use them as an excuse, Aren somehow stopping me from losing my head entirely and screaming my protests at the top of my lungs while he far too politely explained to the guard that my sister needed to return home to nurse her babes. It was the truth; no lies could pass the lips of our kind, and the emperor had accepted it oh-so-graciously.

But I knew. I'd watched as the guard returned to him with the refusal, while Aalia feigned flattery and curtsied so low that her nose practically skimmed the floor and Aren bowed his head in deference to the man who had so casually asked to take his wife to bed. They'd played the game all courtiers had to play and had hidden their true feelings well. But I'd done no such thing. I simply stood and watched that ancient bastard while they played at being willing subjects to his every desire, and I'd seen the way his eyes had flashed with fury at being denied. I'd seen the way he watched Aalia as she was dismissed from his presence, his eyes clinging to her, a possessive intent gripping his features.

I'd begged her to leave this place after that, begged her to take the entire family and head across the empire to the western coast to reunite with our parents if that was what it took to escape the emperor's attention.

But she'd refused me. The world was a big place, filled with more horrors than either of us could count. I knew that, though I had still been keener to brave those horrors than remain and await this one. There were beasts out there, fire and ice drakes who preyed on everything and anything they could make a meal out of, the cruel, dumb cousins to the all-powerful dragons who ruled the deserts.

Then there were the scorpious spiders - enormous, eight-legged monsters with a sting as lethal as their fangs - not to mention wolves, gremlins, the Coy Folk and the Banished. The world beyond the safety of this kingdom was no place for young children, and the passages to other cities of safety were perilous, to say the least. Yet still, I would have run if I could have convinced them to.

But my sister was a stubborn creature when she decided to be, and once her mind was made up, there had been no changing it.

Months had passed, then years, no word from the palace and no demands for Aalia's presence in court. I'd attended once or twice, sticking to the outskirts and observing, wanting to know this enemy I felt lurking in the shadows of our lives, but I had never learned much.

Farish was a cruel ruler when he wanted to be, but he pretended to be a fair one too. There was no denying the power he held though, this entire kingdom was locked in his chokehold, at the mercy of his whims. There was no democracy, nor way to question his law. He played the part of benevolence well but took all he wanted and was denied nothing; a tyrant ruling through brute force. He was old. So old that hardly any Fae remembered a time before his coronation. And he was bored.

I knew well that the oldest of our kind were the most dangerous.

Compassion and kindness were often the first emotions to dwindle in the long lifespan of our people. When a Fae lived through loss, grief, and heartache too many times, they were hardened to it, becoming selfish and petty. Cruel and unyielding.

Aalia's rejection of the emperor had been received simply enough at the time, but it hadn't been forgotten. And her excuse had grown irrelevant too.

"We should think up a reason not to go," I said firmly, beginning to pace as my mind whirled with ideas on what I could do to get her out of this. "A sickness perhaps? I could mix up a tonic which would render you incapable of attending and then-"

"If someone questions what made her sick and discovers what you did, the situation would be far worse," Aren objected, though I could tell he was just as keen as I was to remove Aalia from this obligation.

"I can evade answering easily enough," I replied stubbornly.

"It's too risky. It would be far worse to get caught in a scheme like that. Better we go and try to minimise the damage."

"I can wear that orange gown which you claim makes me look like a pumpkin," Aalia suggested, forcing a smile, and I frowned.

"Nothing can hide your beauty, Aalia. Not truly," I said, a note of fear touching my words.

"We can try," she replied.

I bit my lip as I found myself nodding in agreement. I hated this. Hated every moment of it, but I knew there was no avoiding it. If she didn't appear at court tonight, she would only be summoned again. And again. No one could refuse the command of the emperor and attempting it would likely cause nothing but more harm if it ended up incurring his wrath.

"Fuck," I hissed. "Fine. But I intend to spend the day making you look as unattractive as Faely possible," I swore and at the very least, I got to hear my sister laugh.

# CHAPTER THREE

We stepped out of the carriage which had been sent to collect us and paused in the shadow of the palace, the tips of its many domed roofs gleaming in the sunset as the heat of the day finally began to fade.

There was a long promenade between two perfectly still pools of water which led into the grand entrance of the grotesquely ostentatious building, beautiful flowers blooming in pinks, whites, and yellows from huge golden planters standing on the far edges of them.

Koi of every colour swam slowly through the pools, their movements lazy and progress slow. I eyed them for a moment, wondering if there was any truth to the tales which swore that the emperor owned a pair of vicious crocodiles, bound to his will by one of his advisers whose Affinities gifted her power over animals. Supposedly, the pair resided in those pools, lurking within their mirror-like depths, waiting for the command to strike at any who dared come here with an intent to harm the ruler of our kingdom.

I raised my chin, keeping my shawl close to my body as I looked from the imposing building to the sister I loved more than life itself.

"Kyra," Aalia said slowly, moving closer to me while I inspected the work I'd done to try and downplay her beauty. "What are you planning?"

She wore the orange gown, the colour as close to hideous as any could be on her. It had far too many frills and embellishments, the design gawdy and unfashionable enough that it would likely draw mockery from the spiteful members of the court who followed trends like their lives depended on it. Good. That was good. Let them mock her, and let the emperor hear it too – he prized perfection after all, and I doubted he would wish to be known to bed a woman who had been mocked by the entirety of the court.

Her hair was styled plainly, one overlarge lotus blossom tucked behind her ear, and I had painted her makeup on in a way that tried to diminish her natural beauty, making her cheeks appear a little hollow, her lips sallow, her eyes smaller. Little things which honestly didn't do much to take away from what she was. My sister was beauty incarnate, the Affinity our vain mother had always called a gift and which I had secretly believed to be a curse for some time now.

"Planning?" I echoed innocently, and Aalia's brow furrowed as I avoided the question.

"There's another carriage approaching," Aren murmured, offering an arm to each of us, and I took it, avoiding my sister's gaze as we began the long walk between the pools.

We were quiet as we closed in on the palace, no doubt each as nervous as one another. Because when it came down to it, we knew where this night was likely to lead. The emperor would see Aalia and want her as he had before. He would request her presence once more, and there was no longer a valid excuse beyond the fact that she simply didn't want to accept his offer.

Aalia was pale, and I knew a mixture of fear and acceptance had fallen over her. Acceptance of what she might have to do this night, and perhaps on many more, if the man who ruled our kingdom gained a taste for her. She would do it to protect Aren and the twins. I knew her too well; her heart was too good. She would sacrifice anything for them. But I would not allow it.

Aren was stiff as he walked towards this fate between us, the curve of his bicep beneath my hand rigid where I kept hold of his arm. He was giving everything he could to this façade of calmness and confidence. He was trying to be strong for Aalia, and I was certain that no matter what happened tonight, his love for her wouldn't sway. But I also knew that I wasn't going to let this happen.

I raised my chin as we passed beyond the pools, ignoring the prickling sensation which made me think something watched us pass from beneath that water. Let the crocodiles come for us. I had a feeling they would be the easiest challenge we would face tonight if they did.

A row of twelve royal guards stood at attention either side of the door, their bodies rigid where they clasped their spears, the golden breast plates they wore more decorative than practical, the emperor's crest of two warring dragons emblazoned across the metal. Nothing but their eyes moved as they watched us walk between them into the bright light of the palace.

Servants approached us the moment we stepped inside, one of them asking us to show our invitation. I released my hold on Aren as I finally removed my shawl and handed it to the woman waiting to take it from me.

Aalia sucked in a sharp breath as she took in the entirety of the gown I had chosen to wear tonight, her brown eyes widening as her gaze met mine and accusation filled them.

"No," she hissed, cutting herself off as the servant reached for her shawl next, and I simply gave her a firm look.

Aren ran a hand over his face as comprehension dawned on him too. I found a mixture of grief and gratitude in his eyes as I turned from my sister to him, glad to find that at least one of them understood this.

The gown I wore was a deep scarlet, my lips painted to match the colour, and my ebony hair styled in a way which left most of it hanging loose down my spine. My bare spine. Because though the item I wore was indeed a gown, there was so little of the top half of it that it was entirely scandalous.

"It's the latest fashion," I said blandly to my sister whose cheeks were colouring with her fury at me. It was true enough, though I had opted for the most extreme version of the style, and I didn't back down from the accusation in her eyes as I smoothed out the full-length gossamer skirt and adjusted the delicate golden chains hanging across my midriff beneath the strips of fabric which encircled my neck and crossed over my breasts.

"The fashion may include exposing *some* flesh," Aalia hissed as we headed away down the corridor towards the ballroom where the sounds of music lured us closer. "But you are currently dancing the line of nudity, Kyra."

"So?" I asked innocently, increasing my pace as I leaned into the Affinities which Bentos, the god of seduction and fertility, had given me, my hips swaying with my steps.

A hand gripped my arm and pulled me up short, whirling me back around in the thankfully empty corridor. I arched an eyebrow in surprise as I found Aren holding onto me.

"You mean to take his attention from Aalia?" he asked, pinning me with his dark eyes and forcing an answer from my lips.

"Yes," I replied simply, and Aalia hissed her disapproval.

"I won't let you," she growled, and I turned to look at her, though Aren didn't release his grip on me.

"It's just sex to me, Al," I said, letting her see the truth of that. "I've fucked enough Fae to know the difference between my body and my heart. And if this is the only way to protect you from him, then I will gladly do it."

"I would never ask you to-"

"I know," I interrupted her, tugging my arm free of Aren's grip and moving to clasp her cheek in my palm. "I know you wouldn't. But I would rather spend every night this year in that arsehole's bed than allow your heart to be broken by attending it a single time."

The truth of my words drew a sob to her lips, and she gripped me tightly.

"That doesn't make it okay," she said as I wound my arms around her and let her break for a moment as she accepted this.

"There are two cliffs," I said to her, the story we had both been told so many times by our father, causing a touch of deja-vu to echo around us. "The one you fall off blindly and the one you jump off freely."

"Both hurt when you hit the ground," she replied shakily.

"But I'd always prefer to see my fate coming for me," I finished, pushing her back a step as the sound of more Fae approaching reached us.

"I always picked the blindfold," she muttered, and I smiled, wiping a tear from beneath her eye before looking to Aren.

"I don't want you to do this, Kyra," he began, but I shook my head at him, beckoning them both to start walking again before we were caught lingering here by some nosy courtiers.

"If only we lived in a world where want carried any weight."

Aren offered me his arm again, his hand landing over mine as I took it and squeezed tightly.

"Thank you," he breathed.

I looked up at him and the love and fear I found in his eyes only made my decision on this plan all the easier to accept.

"Who knows?" I teased as we turned a corner and found ourselves before the towering doors to the ballroom. "Perhaps I'll enthral him so deeply that he'll take a queen at last."

Aren scoffed while Aalia choked back a sob, both of them knowing that the life of some pretty queen, dangling from the emperor's arm and enduring court life daily was about as far from the life I would wish for myself as it could get.

The second set of guards bowed low as we passed inside, a herald calling our names and waving a flourishing arm towards the raised dais where the emperor sat on his throne, waiting to greet his guests.

I kept my chin high, my eyes fixed on the emperor while he spoke to one of his advisers, not bothering to so much as look our way. His deep brown hair was slicked back, his jaw rigid and brow broad. Attractive enough, like most of our kind were, but he was no great beauty to look upon. His body was more lean than powerful, his days of practicing with a sword supposedly long forgotten, and I couldn't help but think how terribly average this great and feared emperor was in person. All across the world, people whispered the name of this Fae. Even the rulers of the distant kingdoms and empires didn't dare oppose him too forcefully, and yet there he sat, just another man with too much power and not enough purpose to his endless life.

He was an ancient creature, though time had stopped him from aging at some point in his mid-twenties, as it did to all Fae ever since the gods had blessed us with immortality. But his eyes gave it away. That long life filled with countless nights like this, watching people come and go, enduring endless repetitions and the boredom all the oldest of our kind seemed to indulge in.

I never understood why they didn't just walk on into the Garden. The place beyond. Most did once they reached that point in life, when nothing gave them reason to live anymore, they embraced their end and moved on. But not Emperor Farish. He simply lingered here on his throne, his children watching and waiting for an inheritance I assumed they'd never get. Unless war came to our door and killed him for us.

Farish's head snapped up, his eyes darting to mine and locking with my gaze, making my heart leap. I scoured my mind for any Affinity which might have allowed him to hear that thought, to know that I had just considered his death with not only amusement but anticipation.

Fuck.

I didn't drop his gaze, knowing that all the time his focus remained on me, it wasn't on my sister. But I couldn't think of a single Affinity which might gain a Fae access to the thoughts of another, and I had to hope that my paranoia was simply a side effect of my fear.

"Your Majesty," Aren greeted beside me, his tone warm and submissive as he released his hold on my arm and dipped into a low bow.

Aalia fell into a curtsy beyond him, but I hesitated another second, my gaze still locked with the emperor's. He arched a brow as I danced the line of impertinence before dropping into a low curtsy and murmuring a greeting to him. I didn't lower my gaze though, looking at him while he looked at me and letting him see exactly which powers the gods had gifted me.

He held my gaze for several endless seconds more, and I didn't so much as release my breath until his attention shifted away suddenly, moving over Aren without pause before falling onto my sister.

My heart stilled as the corner of his mouth hitched just the smallest amount, but in the next breath he was waving us away, commanding us to dance and mingle and enjoy the ball, and I was left wondering if I had simply imagined his reaction to her altogether.

We didn't linger, moving quickly to the far side of the ballroom where we endured small talk. I accepted several invitations to dance, my attention never slipping from the emperor while he greeted the rest of the guests.

He didn't look at me or Aalia again, but I couldn't shake the feeling that something was brewing in the air, like an oncoming storm we wouldn't be able to survive.

I wished we hadn't come here. I wished we'd ignored his summons and run. With every turn I took around the dance floor, that feeling increased, like a knot tightening in my stomach until I felt sick with it.

I spun away from my dance partner and gasped as I collided with a hard chest, my gaze rising to meet Calvari's as he took my hand in his and coiled his free arm around my waist, stealing me from my current partner.

"I'm cutting in," he said in a low voice.

The noble, who had looked about to protest, let his gaze roam over the scarred warrior briefly before feigning a sweet smile and graciously abandoning the floor.

"That was rude," I teased as Calvari began to move me. He had less grace than the partner he'd replaced but he knew the steps, and I could admit that I preferred the breadth of his chest to the soft hands of the noble.

"You don't like me for my manners," he replied simply, guiding me across the floor towards Aren and Aalia where they danced together, their eyes on each other and so much emotion in the looks they were sharing that people were starting to comment on it.

"What is it I like you for then?" I teased, and his smile only widened.

He drew my body flush to his, pushing a muscular thigh between my legs with the movement and dipping me backwards as the music quieted for a few beats.

"No need to be vulgar in front of the emperor," Calvari replied, tugging me upright once more.

I caught the grin he threw to the group of warriors who sat at a table not far from the edge of the dance floor and rolled my eyes.

"I thought we didn't do the whole possessive bullshit thing?" I asked as his hand trailed down my bare spine, causing me to arch against him.

"I don't usually," he agreed. "But Ricos seemed to think he had a shot with you. Said you wouldn't look at me twice. Call me an arsehole, but I wanted him to see how fucking wrong he was."

"Ah. So I'm a point to be scored?"

"More like a notch I don't want leaving my belt," he taunted, and I casually swung my knee into his crotch, rising to the bait he was laying while he spun me in a circle and was forced to hide his pain to save face.

"You'll pay for that," I swore to him, drawing half a laugh to his lips even as he continued to curse me.

"Any time, beautiful. You want to tell me what brings you to court though? Can't say I've ever seen you at any of these things before."

As the highest ranking of Farish's army, the elite members of the Fated Warriors were often invited to the palace, brought in to remind everyone of the might the emperor commanded through them. It was hard to miss any of them with their huge frames and glistening weapons, let alone the battle scars, so I understood the posturing, even if it did seem pointless for an emperor who had ruled for longer than most Fae could even remember.

I glanced towards the throne once more, a shard of ice slipping down my spine as I found Farish staring right at me, his gaze boring into the centre of me like he could see all the way down to my soul.

"What's wrong?" Calvari asked, sensing the tension in my posture, his Affinities for war always making him keenly aware of any unrest around him. A Fated Warrior was never caught off guard.

"Nothing," I breathed, but he followed my line of sight, a low chuckle rumbling through his chest.

"The emperor covets all he cannot have," he murmured quietly. "He's noticed the way you're looking at me."

I scoffed, pulling my focus back to Calvari as I arched a brow. "And how is that?"

"Like a woman who knows precisely whose bed she'll be in by dawn."

I began to protest, but Calvari leaned in and grazed my throat with his lips, his hand fisting in my hair as he tugged my head back to give him more room.

I couldn't help it. I looked to the emperor again and, sure enough, his focus was on me.

Fear skittered down my spine and I forced a laugh from my lips, pushing Calvari back a step as I escaped his hold on me and rounded towards the edge of the dance floor. I may have been willing to steal the emperor's attention from my sister if I had to, but I had absolutely no desire to gain it on my own merits.

"I feel a great desire to warm my bed alone tonight," I called loudly as Calvari frowned at me in confusion. "But thank you so much for the offer."

I dipped into a brief curtsy, then let the dancers cut us off from one another before turning and heading to the closest servant holding a tray of sparkling wine.

I needed a drink. More than that, I needed to get far away from the gaze of Emperor Farish.

My heart was racing wildly in my chest, and I had to remind myself that I'd known this could happen, that I had wanted it to happen if it would spare Aalia from his notice. But there was something about the emperor which had always unsettled me, and as I swallowed my wine in one long gulp, I knew without doubt that I held no desire to become his latest plaything.

Let the other jostling court ladies have him. All I wanted was to escape this night with my family and stay away from this place for as long as I could once it was done.

I passed several hours of inane conversation and pitifully tame drinking with one eye on the clock and the other on my sister.

Aalia had clearly relaxed in the time we'd been here, finding herself free of the emperor's gaze and able to enjoy the night dancing with her husband.

I watched them as they twirled around the dancefloor, his gaze riveted to her every move and a smile so pure and beautiful on her face that I swear everyone around them could taste their love for one another in the air they breathed.

It was a connection beyond anyone's ability to deny. Like fated lovers or soulmates, simply meant to be.

I had finally begun to relax too as the final song of the night was struck. I raised a celebratory glass of sweet wine to my lips, but as I looked across the room, I fell still.

Emperor Farish was on his feet, shifting between the crowd on the outskirts of the dance floor like a serpent moving through long grass, somehow going unseen by so many of those who surrounded him.

His guards remained close behind him as he closed in on the dance floor, and I found myself on my feet before I could even be certain of what he was looking at. Because I knew. In the depths of my soul, I knew. And I realised that somehow, despite my vigilance, he had been watching them this entire time too.

I dropped my glass onto a small table without looking, ignoring the sound of it shattering as I broke into a near run, the heels of my shoes clicking against the hard floor as I pushed my way between the bodies. My heart pounded with terror as I ran, my gaze scanning the crowd and finding the large group of warriors among them.

I pushed between the muscular men, ignoring their surprised mutters and grunts of protest. Most of the time, no Fae dared approach a group like theirs, let alone shoved through them, but I wasn't afraid of them, and I had one last chance to stop the roll of fate from landing on my sister's head.

Calvari looked up in surprise from his table, his lips parting on a question, but I simply caught his hand and hauled him to his feet.

"Dance with me," I commanded. "Make the whole world think I'm yours."

The music was just getting to the part where the tempo increased, the song a temptation to sin, the lyrics sung in a language which had been long forgotten but the meanings were clear to any who paid attention to the beat.

This song was written in honour of the god who had blessed me with his Affinities for seduction and allure, and I was going to channel every bit of that energy while there was still time to stop the coin of destiny from falling.

Calvari smirked as he gave in to me, his grip tightening around my fingers before he tugged me close, then spun me away from him fast.

My feet moved with the natural agility of our kind, my skirt flaring and parting around my thighs as I spun onto the dance floor. Before I could stop my spinning, Calvari was there again, catching my hand and yanking me back to him.

My palms landed hard against his chest as he caught my hips and lifted me, the heat which had flared between us last night building as I kicked my legs back into the air before swinging forward and winding them around his waist.

This kind of dancing was what had first brought us to one another, the unfettered, feral kind which came straight from the depths of the soul and simply had to be set free.

The solstice party we'd met at so many years ago almost seemed to reappear around us, the depth of the night and the heat of the bonfire in the sand, while the summer breeze tangled with my hair and we danced without limitations in the heart of the desert.

Our bodies moved to the same rhythm, his hand locking around my throat as he drew my mouth almost close enough to kiss me and then spun me away sharply, turning me beneath his arm as my skirt whirled once more.

He yanked me back to him, my spine to his chest as I dropped down low then rose up again.

People were watching us; I could feel their eyes following our movements hungrily, and more than a few Fae moved out onto the dance floor to join in. Those who felt the call of Bentos' power just as I did.

I could feel the allure of the god as he drew closer too, this dance a form of worship to the one who had blessed us with his power.

My skin heated and desire flushed my cheeks, the friction of Calvari's body against mine riling me up and making me hunger for more.

His hands moved over my body, possessive, controlling, worshipping, and as I whipped around, I found exactly what I had been aiming to achieve.

Emperor Farish was staring right at us, his dark eyes ripping through my skin as easily a hot knife shearing through butter.

I held his gaze as I ground my body against Calvari's, biting into my bottom lip with a promise sparkling in my golden eyes.

His nostrils flared just slightly, his head tipping to one side as he muttered a word to his Royal Prophet, Kalir, and I tried not to look towards the shadows within the hood of those ice-white robes.

I almost missed a step as Calvari's mouth brushed the side of my neck, but I refused to allow a moment of fear to colour my actions. Kalir was an atrocity so far as I was concerned, and the magic he wielded was nothing but stolen energy from the gods. It was an affront to the power and lives they had gifted us to steal from them the way his kind did.

There were many who muttered fears that the Prophets would one day curse us all for what they took, the sorcery they wielded which was unnatural and unearned. They were capable of far more than the power of our Affinities, but the cost it reaped upon their souls was clear to see the moment they dropped those white hoods.

I had no idea why the emperor kept a man like that so close to him, and the thought of Kalir turning his attention to me for so much as a moment made a prickle of terror spear through me, despite my best intentions.

I forced my focus back to Emperor Farish just as Calvari dropped his hands to my hips and dipped me backwards. I gave my body to him, my spine arching as he whirled me around, my thighs locking around his waist before he tugged me upright once more and our bodies were pressed together again.

My head turned to the emperor, but Calvari caught my jaw and snapped my gaze back to his, the cocky smirk on his lips letting me know that he had figured out my game.

The music was racing towards its crescendo, and Calvari's hand moved to encircle my throat as he tilted my mouth up towards his.

"Trying to bed yourself an emperor, are you?" he purred against my lips, a mixture of amusement and jealousy in his words as his eyes flashed with the challenge of fighting for my attention.

"Perhaps," I breathed, watching as his pupils dilated and his grip on my throat tightened.

He drew me closer, not a breath between our bodies as he lowered my left foot to the floor but gripped my right thigh tightly, keeping it at his hip, our position beyond indecent and the world still watching.

Calvari leaned in, his mouth set to capture mine and the heat in my skin begging for him to do so.

"Enough!" Emperor Farish clapped his hands together once and the music fell silent.

A beat passed as Calvari kept hold of me, his nostrils flaring at the command to stop while the heat of that dance and his own desire made him reluctant to do so.

With a barely concealed curse, Calvari released his grip on me, lowering my right foot to the ground before taking his hand from my throat and stepping back with a harsh exhale.

I bit my bottom lip as I turned to look at the emperor, certain that I'd had his attention, that he had seen Calvari's claim on me and that it would be enough. Because it had to be enough.

I didn't dare turn to look for my sister as we all awaited the emperor's next words, and his dark eyes slowly surveyed the gathered courtiers like a wolf in the midst of a flock of sheep, simply taking his time while he selected a meal.

His gaze fell to me, and I fought my natural instinct to recoil as his heated attention roamed over my body, taking in every exposed piece of skin, the way my chest rose and fell from the dance, everything right down to the flush in my cheeks. He glanced at Calvari too, a smile almost touching his lips which seemed as close to a challenge as I could imagine.

The warrior at my side stared back defiantly for several seconds before bowing his head in submission and taking a step away from me. An offer. One which shouldn't have stung but did just a little.

There had never been any promises between the two of us, but there had been something. Or perhaps I had only wanted to let myself think that.

Either way, he was offering me up without protest, and I had to remind myself that that was precisely what I had been aiming for anyway.

A smugness filled the emperor's expression as he looked between the two of us, and my heart began to race as his gaze slid over me and then away, beyond me, looking through the crowd and seeking out the woman who I had tried so hard to shield from him.

There was a flash of cruelty that flared in his eyes as his gaze fell on my sister where she held her husband's hand, her eyes lowered in hopes of going unnoticed. An excitement filled Farish's expression that surpassed any lust he might have felt for me.

I saw it then. Saw the truth of this man who sat above all of us on a throne which he had laid claim to for a thousand years, making the world bow to his whims.

This wasn't about sex. It wasn't lust and pleasure between the thighs of a beautiful woman he sought. I'd had him in my thrall, he had seen me, and he had known what my Affinities were, known what I was capable of if he had invited me to his bed. If he simply wanted sex, the rough, brutal act of fucking for the sake of nothing but pleasure, then he could have turned his attention from her. But that wasn't it. This was about power. It was as much about her love for Aren and her children as it was about her beauty.

He could fuck any number of beautiful women, and no doubt had over the centuries as often and as endlessly as he pleased. But in that time, this creature who called himself our emperor had grown bored of simply taking his pick of willing bodies. So he'd created this game. One where he used his power to take what wouldn't be willingly offered without duress. One where he could make a man relinquish his wife for a night or many nights if he pleased, where he could watch his conquests' hearts break as they gave themselves up to him out of fear of what might happen if they refused. One where he could taste the pain and destruction on the lips he stole kisses from.

He raised his hand slowly, extending a single finger as he pointed Aalia out in the crowd and lazily, almost as if this were boring him, he beckoned her to him.

## CHAPTER FOUR

T he ground seemed to buck beneath my feet as I turned to stare at my sister in horror, wanting to scream at her to run or fight or do anything at all other than move to the emperor's command.

I had a feeling of dread in the pit of my stomach that wouldn't shift. This deep and unending knowledge that with that one single action, Emperor Farish had shifted her fate beyond control.

I didn't know what to do. I didn't know how I could help her, but I could sense the power I had been born with manifesting inside of me like a roiling storm cloud, ready to unleash hell on the world as we knew it.

I took a single step, uncertain what I even intended, but before I could make that decision, Calvari had me in his arms, my back to his chest as he locked me against him and growled a low warning in my ear.

I began to struggle, willing to kick him in his manhood if that was what it took to make him release me, but before I could do any such thing, my sister spoke.

"May I ask why you are summoning me, Your Highness?" Aalia asked, her voice outwardly calm, though I still detected that faint note of fear in it as Aren squeezed her hand tightly in his.

The room took a collective breath, every Fae in attendance stiffening as if in anticipation of a blow. I wasn't sure I had even heard of anyone questioning the motives of the emperor before that moment, and I honestly had no idea how he might respond.

I looked to Farish, my entire body tensed as if expecting a blow to land.

Farish blinked slowly, almost as though he were uncertain of what had just happened, perhaps so unused to anyone doing anything other than following his commands without protest that he wasn't even sure how to react.

Kalir stepped forward before he had to though, his white robes swirling around him as he pushed his hood back and revealed the shaved head beneath and harsh features, his eyes glowing with that stolen power, and the air itself crackling in reply to the anger in his expression.

"You have been selected to service the gods' chosen ruler of our kingdom," Kalir snarled. "Would you question the word of the divine beings themselves so casually?"

"She has a husband," I called out, forcing the sorcerer's attention onto me even as Calvari continued to restrain me. "She pledged her life and body to him in the temples of each and every one of them when their union was decided. Would you have her go back on her word to them? Though I suppose to a man who steals from the magic of the gods themselves and twists the natural power of this earth to his unholy methods, a broken oath is of little consequence."

"For the love of Saresh, hold your tongue," Calvari hissed in my ear as I struggled to free myself of his hold. "Do you want to find your head struck from your body in the middle of this ballroom?"

I ignored his warning as I continued to try and break free of his grip, Kalir looking like I had just slapped his face and told the entire kingdom his cock had fallen off for good measure.

"How dare you question a member of the royal court in the heart of the palace itself-" Kalir began in outrage, but before he could go on with his tirade and act on those murderous thoughts I could see swirling in his unnaturally bright eyes, the emperor spoke.

"Enough," he said firmly, his eyes moving from me to Aalia, then to Aren, nothing at all in his expression to say what he might do or command next, but that terror was still eating into my gut, a scream sounding at the edge of my comprehension which warned me to run and run and run. "If the lady wishes to keep the vows she made before the gods to her husband, then so be it. I grow weary of this debate. Tell me, *Aalia*, is it your intention to deny my request for your company and return home with your husband this night?"

I fell still in Calvari's grasp, my heart thundering so loudly that I was sure the entire court could hear it even as all eyes turned to my sister in search of her answer.

Aalia was deathly pale as she clung to Aren's hand, her husband taking half a step forward, as if wishing to place himself between her and the wrath the emperor might impose upon her for this public insult.

"Yes," she breathed eventually, her voice so low I barely caught the word, but the gasps of shock and outrage that fluttered through the crowd like wind through stalks of wheat made it all too clear.

Emperor Farish let his gaze trail down her body so slowly that even I squirmed from the intensity of his assessment, before a smile tugged his lips into what seemed like a mockery of amusement, and he simply waved a hand at them.

"Then go."

I didn't even feel Calvari release me, I just ran for my sister, my high heels clacking loudly against the hard floor and the Fae of the court parting for me like they didn't want to so much as touch me in case they were tarred with the same brush as our family had just been.

Aren was already turning away, tugging Aalia after him, but she kept her eyes on me as I raced to them, ignoring the stern look I was giving her and resisting Aren's grip until I reached her.

I grabbed her other arm and we hurried from the ballroom, picking up a fast pace as we headed down the dimly lit stone corridors towards the exit without a word passing between us.

I expected to hear the sound of soldiers taking chase, or even a simple command for us to stop, but none came, and we hurried out of the palace, past the now-empty guard post.

Unease rolled through me as the sense of pursuit failed to ease, and we wordlessly broke into a run between the two still pools of water before the palace, needing to escape as fast as we could.

I prayed to every god I could think of for their protection, glancing back over my shoulder expectantly while my mind scoured my knowledge of the gods as I tried to think up a bargain any of them might enter into for our safety. The gods were fickle creatures, their attention shifting from place to place without warning, few of them ever answering the desperate pleas of their followers. But there was one who was rumoured to offer up deals readily, one who was willing to trade with anyone desperate enough to risk his price.

And I was desperate. Because despite the unnatural silence and apparent disinterest in our departure, I knew better. We were running out of time, and something was fast coming our way.

"Carioth, I'll give you anything you ask if you can help us escape this place," I hissed to the god of tricksters and cunning as the water in the pools either side of us began to stir. Something huge shifted within their depths, drawing closer with every moment, and I could only hope the god was listening and would take the bargain I offered.

Aalia gasped in fear as the water continued to churn, the beasts rumoured to slumber in under the surface waking to hunt us down while we ran past their watery domains like all-too-easy prey.

For a moment, I thought the god was ignoring my pleas, but as we broke into an all-out sprint, a charge of powerful energy rushed through the air, something shifting before us as the shadows deepened beyond the end of the pools.

Aalia screamed, and I followed her gaze to our right where an enormous shape was taking form within the water, the flowers which had sat so prettily on its surface shifting away as the thing drew closer.

My Affinities swelled within me, magic coursing through my blood, but I seriously doubted a dose of powerful healing magic was going to do anything against the fucking monsters which were chasing us through the dark.

A faint note of laughter caught on the breeze, and I looked towards the thickening darkness again as I felt the presence of a god drawing closer, Carioth come to answer my prayers.

*"One kiss from the lips that betrayed you, one smile for your time in the dark, a scream for the monsters which plague you, a debt paid to he with the mark."* The voice of the god tangled with the wind, teasing fingers through my hair and pouring starlight through my veins.

I gasped at the weight of his power, feeling his presence so keenly that I stumbled. The shadows ahead of us thickened further, but my gaze snapped straight to a spot in the heart of them where two bright green eyes watched us with amusement flickering in their depths.

"We have a bargain!" I cried, unable to take my time deciphering his price as the water to our right exploded with motion, a crocodile larger than I even could have imagined launching itself at us with its jaws wide and a bellow of murderous intent breaking from its mouth.

Aalia screamed again, and Aren tried to throw himself between her and the beast, but a collar of pure starlight lashed around its neck before the crocodile's jaws could snap closed, and it was yanked to a jarring halt just out of reach of the three of us.

I stumbled aside, falling to the hard tiles as I stared at the dark green monster in horror. It thrashed against the leash while the laughter of the god of tricksters filled the air and made goosebumps rise all over my skin, his power containing the furious creature like it was little more than a naughty puppy tugging at its leash.

Aren's hand locked around my arm and he yanked me to my feet, shoving me ahead of him towards the waiting darkness.

I didn't look back as I chased after my sister, the orange gown she wore billowing around her as she sprinted for the promise of safety within those shadows ahead. My skin prickled with awareness as Aren shoved me in front of him, my pulse hammering wildly.

My mind shifted to the other pool, the other crocodile which was yet to appear and the fate which could leap out at us at any moment, terror threatening to consume me.

But as we ran for the darkness, it seemed to reach for us too, those bright green eyes watching with hungry amusement until the tendrils of shadow coiled around us and swallowed us whole.

I called Aalia's name as she was consumed by the dark, reaching for her in the abyss and gasping as a rough hand met with mine, tugging me against an impossibly broad chest while wicked laughter filled the air.

*"Run, run, little rabbit,"* Carioth purred, the incredible energy which he was made of stealing the breath from my lungs.

I tipped my head back to look up at him, trying to make out the face of the god among the endless shadow. But all I could see of him were those bright green eyes, full of mirth and wicked cunning. Then he smiled, his teeth blazing white and razor sharp between lips I couldn't perceive.

My instinct was to recoil, to scream or beg for mercy, but I had never been the cowering kind and our bargain had already been struck.

"You owe us an escape," I demanded, my gaze fixing on his.

The power of that bargain hummed in the air around us and Carioth began to laugh in that cruel and taunting way of his again. The sound rattled through me, through the world itself, but even as I ached to cover my ears and hide from it, I felt his hands tighten around my arms as he pushed me back.

My knees hit with the edge of a seat and I was forced to sit, finding soft cushions beneath me as a warm hand gripped mine, and I recognised my sister with a cry of relief.

"Kyra?" Aren's voice came from directly opposite us, and I confirmed that it was me while craning my head to look around us, fighting to see through the darkness.

A lurch of movement made me grip the edge of my seat, and the thunder of hooves met with the roiling movement of the carriage as we began to speed away from the palace.

The darkness lifted as we raced through the palace gates and into the city beyond, shadows peeling off of us and tumbling away on the wind. The carriage was made of some kind of obsidian stone, the four huge wheels creaking and thumping as they rotated along the ground at impossible speed, making my gut lurch with the movement.

I gripped Aalia's hand tighter, offering her a reassuring smile as the world raced by incredibly fast around us.

Carioth's laughter drew my attention to the god where he sat in the front of the carriage, driving us away from peril and cracking a long whip at the creatures which pulled it. My lips parted as I took in the four enormous hyenas, one of them swinging its head around to grin at me like it felt my attention and wanted me to look.

I knew I should have felt more fear then, but perhaps I had run out of terror following our escape, or perhaps I had lost my mind, because there was something in the gaze of that beastly animal which called to me. Its eyes were dark and full of secrets, bursting with the knowledge of a thousand lifetimes visiting every corner of the world. These were the steeds of a god, powerful, wonderous creatures who had tasted adventure every second of their being. And all it took was that single look to let me know they had loved each and every moment of it and promised me that I would too, if only I took the leap to find it for myself.

Everyone had heard the tales of the shadow chariot owned by the trickster god, pulled by four beasts of cunning and irreverence, but I had never in my life believed I might see it for myself, nor that I might find myself wishing for the life of a beast serving at the whims of a deity, but here I was. And it felt a whole lot like everything I'd been aching for my entire life.

We shot through the streets at breakneck speed, the three of us carried towards safety in the hands of a god. And despite the utter insanity we found ourselves in, and the possible repercussions which could be heading our way, I started laughing right along with Carioth.

Laughing and fucking laughing to the balmy night air as we stole through the dark in a chariot of shadows pulled by a pack of monsters. Because despite everything, we were free.

# CHAPTER FIVE

"*A memory of fear and destruction, a piece of you lost to corruption.*" The words twisted through me in the darkness of my mind before tumbling away into nothing once more, lost on a tide of laughter which was powered by a creature far beyond my ability to understand.

I groaned as I woke, my eyes reluctant to peel apart as I kicked the sheets from my bare legs and tried to get my bearings.

I was in my bed, sleep clinging to my limbs as I rolled over and looked towards the curtains which billowed by the open balcony doors in a breeze warm enough to let me know that it was rolling in from the desert.

Sweat clung to my skin and I felt uneasy, like something was wrong, but I couldn't tell what.

I pushed myself upright, sweeping the length of my tangled black hair away from my face as I tried to figure out what was disturbing me. It was like a memory I couldn't quite grasp, or a thought I had forgotten in light of another pushing its way into my head.

I got to my feet, moving towards the balcony and pulling the long curtain aside as I looked out into the gardens, listening to the familiar burble of the stream and letting the calmness of this place wash over me. The feeling of dread faded, and I exhaled a long breath to expel the last of my anxiety.

No doubt I'd had another nightmare, one of the temples falling and the gods cursing us.

I wasn't even certain when the dreams had begun, only that the taste of prophecy lingered on my tongue when I woke, along with that metallic essence which reminded me of the weakness plaguing all of our kind. Iron. The metal the gods wielded so easily and which held such power over each of the Fae. A simple touch from it could render us nauseous, manacles restraining our power and bringing our bodies to the point of utter weakness. I'd heard once that a coffin built of it could put a Fae to sleep for a thousand years, immortality clinging to their limbs and leaving them in suffering the entire time. Suffice to say, it wasn't something I thought of fondly.

I shook my head as I dropped the curtain, moving to the bathing chamber and finding a steaming bath already drawn for me, flowers floating on the surface and making me fall still abruptly.

I blinked at the flowers, my heart racing as I fought the urge to recoil, like I was half expecting something to burst from the water and attack me, though I couldn't place the reason for my fear.

Faint laughter pricked at my ears, and I spun, muscles tensing as I searched for the owner of that voice, even as the note of mirth faded away.

"Hello?" I called, wondering if the children were close by, playing tricks on me as they often liked to do. But no reply came, no guilty giggling or pattering of little feet to identify the culprits, and a chill ran down my spine.

I wetted my lips, glancing around like I might see something out of place, but the birds were singing outside, the heat of the day rising steadily and nothing at all suggesting that anything might be wrong.

I tried to shake off the sensation, shedding my nightgown and sinking into the heated bath.

Water sloshed over my head as I submerged myself fully, holding my breath as I remained under for a count of fifty. It was something I'd done since I was a child, hiding beneath the water and pretending the entire world had disappeared beyond me, that everything I knew was gone, lost forever, and when I emerged it would be into a new world. One that was terrifying and utterly different to all I had ever known, full of strange wonders and terrifying beasts, temptations and miracles, terror, and adventure deep within the eyes of a stranger whose face I couldn't see and whose name I couldn't summon. But I felt like he was waiting for me, just out of reach somewhere in a future I had no idea how to find.

A pretty daydream for a girl who had never quite fit where she'd been born.

I stayed beneath the water after the count of fifty, my lungs straining, clarity beckoning to me through the shafts of light which punctured my watery refuge, an answer to a question which I hadn't even asked yet floating down there with me.

Eyes watched me from within that light. Dark eyes drenched in sin, hungry for all the world had to offer and looking to take full ownership of my destiny.

"Who are you?" I asked, the last of my oxygen escaping my lips in a stream of bubbles.

My answer was a smirk which made my heart flip over itself and words which I wasn't even certain I had heard at all. *"Not yet, little goddess."*

I lurched for the surface, gasping loudly as I sucked down air, my fingers biting into the edges of the tub while my heart thundered in my chest and a crackling energy coursed through the entire room. That metallic taste coated my tongue, the tell-tale sign of prophecy making me wonder at the stranger who might be waiting for me in the time to come.

"Whoa, Kyra, why are you flooding the bathing chamber?" Aalia laughed as she stepped into the room, and relief consumed me as I found her there, like I'd been expecting something bad to happen to her, only to find her safe after all.

"Are you alright?" I asked, reaching for her hand, and she gave me a frown as she let me take it, squeezing my fingers in hers.

"Why wouldn't I be?" she asked.

Her words made my brows pinch with confusion before I shook my head to disperse it, relaxing back against the tub and forcing myself to release my hold on her.

"I don't know...perhaps the gods are playing with me this morning," I muttered, swiping a hand over my face. "I feel like I'm forgetting something important. Or like I have somewhere to be."

"Well, I need to run into town later to buy some new shoes for the twins, they're growing out of the ones they have already. Maybe you're thinking you should come with me and keep me company? But it's Thursday so..." Aalia teased, and I groaned, knowing I couldn't do that.

"I have clinic today," I realised with a sigh. "And after that sandstorm cut last week's short, I'm bound to be run off my feet."

I didn't really begrudge the work I did, offering up my healing skills to anyone who needed my assistance. As one of the most powerful Fae in the city with my healing Affinity, it was both an honour and a duty to do so – though most in my position required coin for the work they did. I preferred to offer my gifts out charitably to those who couldn't afford the steep prices the other healers charged. More than a few of my peers sneered at me for the lost fortune, but my family was wealthy beyond any needs I would ever have, and I wouldn't see the poorest of our kind suffering through ill health and injury out of a desire for wealth I didn't need. I loved my work, but it also drained me to the point of exhaustion, especially on a busy day like this one would no doubt be.

"They've already begun to queue in the outer courtyard," Aalia admitted. "The servants were putting the awnings out and fetching pitchers of water."

"Okay." I reached for the tonic to wash my hair, but Aalia took it before I could, moving around the tub and massaging it into my scalp for me.

I lay there among the scented water and flowers, my eyes closed as she washed my hair for me, and I stole a few moments of calm before the chaos of my day could begin in earnest.

"All done," Aalia announced far too soon.

I forced myself to rise, drying off and dressing in a loose-fitting pair of harem pants with a thin top to match, my midriff bare and the navy material light enough to help combat the heat. Though I could already tell it would be relentless today.

"Eat," Aalia said firmly, passing me a sweet bun which Aren had no doubt made, as I emerged from the bathing chamber, and I bit into it with a grin.

"Has Aren taken the twins to visit his parents?" I asked through a mouthful as we both began to head downstairs, the comfortable companionship I only ever fully felt with her a welcome reprieve from the unease I'd woken to.

"Yes. They left first thing, and I'll join them for dinner when I'm done at the market. Unless you need me here?" she offered, but I was already shaking my head.

"Imra and the others will be here soon, if they're not already," I said. "You go and enjoy your day. No doubt Aren has left plenty of snacks to get us through the chaos."

Aalia nodded in confirmation, this routine familiar to us after years of practicing it. Aren always prepared several kinds of delicious baked goods and left them close to the various work stations in the dining hall where I held my clinics. Imra and six other Fae with lesser healing Affinities came to help me run them, learning from me and taking over with the simpler cases. None of them had the power I did, but they were all sharp-witted and quick on their feet, the group of us forming a well-oiled unit. But it was hard to take time out for proper meals while we worked, so the bite-sized treats Aren prepared for us got us through the day.

Aren and Aalia took the twins to visit with his parents on clinic days to save them from getting underfoot and keep them from seeing some of the grizzlier maladies. My doors were always open in an emergency, but many Fae waited if they weren't desperate for a remedy and turned up to clinic with festering wounds or abbesses, burns or boils; and the unfiltered questions of young children weren't ideal in those situations.

We made it to the foot of the stairs and Aalia drew me into her arms, squeezing me briefly before making a move to pull away, but a flash of terror ripped through me and I lurched for her, gripping her hard and drawing her back into my arms.

"Wait..." I gasped, trailing off when the thought which had almost formed on my tongue slipped from me, and I was left frowning at her as she looked back at me with equal confusion.

"What is it?" Aalia asked, but I just shook my head, certain there had been something even as I failed to figure out what it was.

"I just...need you to be safe," I said slowly, a distant note of laughter making me turn my head and look back up the stairs.

I sucked in a sharp breath as I spotted a figure there, but as I released Aalia and whirled towards it, I found nothing but dust motes swirling in a beam of sunlight.

"Kyra?" Aalia questioned, but my frown deepened as I failed to understand what I'd seen...or hadn't seen.

"I thought..."

I looked back to her, blinking firmly to clear my mind, and she reached out to cup my face in her hand.

"Did you sleep poorly?" she asked, and I shrugged.

"Maybe. Something just feels off today. Doesn't it?"

Aalia began to disagree but then she frowned down at her hands, holding them out between us for a moment before dropping them again.

"I had the strangest feeling of weakness when I woke," she said slowly. "Like I'd been fighting to push something away from me, but I couldn't. I felt like I couldn't breathe-"

"And?" I asked, a hush falling around us even though I knew I'd been able to hear Imra and the others setting up in the dining hall just a moment ago.

"I woke to a child leaping on me." She laughed, the moment of tension falling away as she shrugged. "Perhaps the gods are toying with us today, like you said."

I nodded vacantly, glancing back at the top of the stairs as that feeling of dread tried to resurface again, but Aalia simply pressed a kiss to my cheek and turned away.

"There are two cliffs, Kyra," she called cheerfully, and though a part of me churned with the desire to race after her and stop her from leaving, I couldn't think of a single reason to do so.

"I'll jump blindly," I replied automatically, and her laugh was cut off as the door closed behind her.

My last vision of her was with the sunlight gilding her hair and a bright smile on her face as she lifted her chin to the sky before walking away.

I took a step towards the door, the urge to call her back to me rising once more, but the sound of my name drew my attention towards the dining hall as Imra came rushing out of it.

"We have a boy who was hit by a carriage," she said, the look in her eyes telling me it was bad even as she maintained that calm composure we all knew was so important to our work.

"Okay," I said, hurrying to follow her.

But even as my gaze fell on the boy and I hurried into action to try and save his life, a little voice in the back of my head was screaming at me to chase after my sister and call her back inside.

# CHAPTER SIX

The day and most of the night had passed in a blur of constant action, and my limbs trembled with fatigue as we worked to clear through the final patients. Imra was the last of the healers left with me, the others having headed out over the final hours of the evening to make some house calls and deliver tonics to the Fae who hadn't been able to show up in person.

As I turned to cross the room, the toe of my shoe caught on a flagstone and I stumbled, catching the arm of a man who I hadn't even seen.

"Sorry," I muttered, righting myself and pulling back, frowning as I looked up into his face and took in the uniform of one of the city guards. "Are you here for the clinic?"

"No. I'm not here for myself. We found… There has been an incident which I'm sorry to have to inform you of, but this is the Dumari household, is it not?"

"Yes," I replied hesitantly, looking beyond the guard and spotting another lurking in the doorway, his gaze hard as he looked around the room at the few remaining patients. "What is it you want?"

"Are the Lord and Lady home currently-"

"My parents have been travelling the continent for several years. My sister and I act on behalf of the estate in their absence," I told him. "What is it?"

Fatigue tugged at my mind like it was laced in cotton wool and the words he spoke were but distant things. I was tired. Right down to my bones, I felt drained of both physical and godly energy. There had been more than a few difficult cases today, and so much use of my Affinities always wore on me. No doubt I'd remain in bed for the entire next day and likely part of the one after to recover.

The guard cut a look to Imra, and my friend took the hint, dipping into the barest suggestion of a curtsy before heading across the room to finish bandaging a man with a broken arm. I'd used my power to help the bone fuse back together, but he needed to keep it still for a week while the bone hardened again.

"This way," the guard inclined his head, and I followed as he led me from the room, tossing the cloth I'd been using to clean my hands into a bucket by the door as we went.

The torches which had been lit along the main hall had burned low and darkness pressed in on me as I followed the two guards along it, their heavy steps echoing in the empty space while mine stayed silent against the flagstones.

I swallowed a lump in my throat as we walked, each step we took towards the courtyard to the front of the manor house seeming to clear a haze from around me, and I jolted in alarm as a voice hissed in my ear.

*"One kiss from the lips that betrayed you, one smile for your time in the dark, a scream for the monsters which plague you, a debt paid to he with the mark."* Carioth's voice made my feet trip over themselves, and I stumbled forward, hardly even noticing as one of the guards caught my arm to stop me from falling, let alone hearing the words he spoke to me.

I righted myself, whirling to look back down the long corridor into the heart of the house, a breath of laughter weaving through the air which had the guards cursing behind me just as I spotted a pair of bright green eyes.

I opened my mouth to demand an answer from the god of tricksters but before the words could spill from my lips, a curtain seemed to lift from my mind, memories rushing in so fast that they stole my breath, and my heart began to race so quickly that I pressed a hand to it in fright.

"Why are you here?" I demanded of the god, feeling like a fool as my mind raced over everything that had happened last night. Everyone knew Carioth was the most likely of the gods to strike a bargain with a Fae, and in my desperation, I'd called on him. But he was also the god of stealth and cunning, a trickster who delighted in messing with the rules of the deals he struck, and as my memories came crashing in, I realised with terror what he had done, how he'd stolen them and stolen our chance to flee too.

He had helped us escape like our bargain demanded, but he had also made us forget what we'd been running from. We shouldn't have lingered in the city. All of us should have fled the moment we were free of the palace and never looked back, but instead we'd remained here, gone about our days as if nothing at all had even-

"We found her in an alley in Rower's Bay," said the guard who was still holding my arm, answering the question I had intended for the god.

Ice water spilled through my veins at his words, my head shaking in denial even as I struggled to put them together.

"It ain't a part of the city where noble ladies tend to go," the second guard muttered. "We were thinkin' maybe she had business of an unsavoury nature over that way. Or perhaps she was there for a clandestine liaison-"

"No," I breathed in horror, yanking my arm free of the guard, and looking beyond him, my eyes falling on the open carriage waiting there, the covered shape which lay in the back of it looking all too still.

"Maybe you can shed some light on why she went out that way-"

I wasn't listening to them anymore. There was a ringing in my ears which was drowning them out and the pounding in my chest was so violent that my ribs seemed in danger of cracking from the force of each pounding thump.

My feet began to move as dread sliced me open and left me bleeding out with every single step I took.

A shaft of moonlight pierced the sky to land directly over the carriage, marking the spot in pale light which defied the press of the dark.

Inside my head, the voice of a little girl was screaming, begging me not to take a single step further. The voice of the child I had been, the one who had played in the long grass outside the family manor with Aalia day after day, creating imaginary worlds to explore and speaking of all the things we would venture out into the world to see when we were grown.

She was crying now, sobbing and begging, while on the outside I didn't so much as flinch. It was as if my skin had set to stone, my expression halted in a mask of absolute nothingness as I fought the urge to believe what my heart already knew.

It couldn't be.

There wasn't any light in a world without her.

The carriage seemed so innocuous, just a simple wooden structure lined with hay and drawn by a single black horse who looked tired and ready for a return to his stable.

My hand trembled as I reached for the blanket covering what lay in the back of it, my throat thickening as that voice in my head kept screaming and screaming, the force of her fear ripping through me like I might tear in two and become half of the person I was if I didn't heed her denial.

But the cold, hard statue which had taken control of my flesh didn't slow, didn't stop.

My fingers reached the edge of the blanket, and I choked as I felt the coldness of the body laying beneath the rough fibres. The unnatural stillness that met with my touch.

My fingers knotted in the rough fabric, my heart racing, racing, racing so fast that the pounding in my ears almost drowned out those screams.

I yanked it hard, the blanket tearing free of her and catching on the air as it fell all too softly to the ground.

It shouldn't have been soft. It should have caused a thunderclap which ripped through the world and set it all alight with the power of the grief that stole through me as my gaze fell upon her.

"Aalia," I choked out, my shin slicing open on the edge of the carriage as I hauled myself onto it, that screaming ripping through me, tearing me open from the inside out while I scrambled for her, shaking my head in denial of what I saw.

The guards were talking but there was no noise which could reach me in the fog of grief echoing through my core at the sight of her beautiful face, too pale in the moonlight, lips swollen with bruises, a slit through the lower like she'd taken a strike to the face.

The screams broke free of me, pouring from my lungs in an unending wail of denial and despair as I reached for her, pressing my hands to her cool cheeks, and willing every ounce of power I possessed to rise up inside of me and reverse this fate.

I hauled her into my arms, her body a limp weight as I heaved her into my lap and screamed her name.

The collar of her dress parted as I begged for her to return to me, her beauty only accentuated in death as the moonlight cast her stunning features into stark perfection. There were bruises on her, dark, purple bruises which ringed her neck like a collar, the outline of hands far bigger than mine marring her skin and providing the reason for her demise.

My anguish turned to horror as I realised my own blame in this, the day we should have spent escaping lost to us through Carioth's tricks and the cold bite of reality.

Power rattled through me as I called on all I had and tried to offer it to her. I was a healer, blessed by Luciet herself with the power to ward off death.

"Please," I choked out between sobs, that power in me growing as I tried to use all I had for the benefit of my sister, offering it all if only her body could heal from this.

Silver light grew on the edges of my vision, and I knew the goddess was watching me, I could feel her grief compounding with mine as she felt the raw brutality of this loss, but she did nothing to change it. Because it was already far too late for the power of a healer, far, far too late for my magic, or even the power of the goddess who had bestowed it upon me, to have any affect.

Tears spilled free of me then as my screams tore through the darkness of the night.

"Take me," I begged, my mind slipping to those precious souls who needed my sister even more than I did. Her beautiful twins, the light of her world and mine alike, waiting for her to return. "Herdat hear me, and take me in her place. Her children need her, please take this trade."

Her body was so cold in my arms, so still and void of life, everything she had been so far removed from what was left of her here.

My soul was shredded apart, my heart destroyed and mind cracking as I screamed to the gods for mercy, for pity, for anything and everything I could, begging them each by name before offering myself up to Herdat over and over again, my Affinities burning so bright that my skin glowed with the useless power of them.

But the goddess of death and ruin did not rise to my pleas, did not answer my request, and no matter how potent my own power was, I was no match for death itself.

## CHAPTER SEVEN

I knelt on the cold floor of the temple of Herdat, goddess of death and ruin, my sister's body laying before me on the stone altar, her hair brushed to a shine, her silver dress accentuating her beauty beyond all denial and the low neckline letting the entire world see what had been done to her if they cared to look.

The time that had passed since her death had been an agony unlike anything I had ever known.

People had come to mourn her, speaking words of loss and despair over a woman they had never truly known. Not like I had. Not like Aren and her twins had.

Something inside me had splintered and shorn off. A piece which would never return because it had been so intrinsically linked to her that it couldn't exist without her to breathe life into it.

I felt cold. Deep down to the roots of my core, cold. Like frost had taken root in the part of my soul which demanded I keep living beyond her death. It was growing inside me, climbing through my veins and freezing everything it touched, kissing my lips so that they forgot how to smile, chilling my eyes so they forgot how to cry, and stilling my heart so that it only beat in shallow, insignificant thumps which did nothing beyond staving off death.

Because I didn't want to die.

Not yet.

I wanted to claim my revenge first.

Inside me, a little girl still screamed and raged at the world, her broken heart whispering words to me between thoughts, giving me a taste of her pain whenever she could with the lash of her tongue against the inside of my skull. She was me and not me. Fractured, divided. Like I had split in two but remained in one body.

*You made that bargain,* she hissed with venom, the memory of Carioth's acid green eyes haunting me from within my own mind. *You let her leave the house that day.*

"I know," I told myself, because I wasn't denying it. Aalia's death fell on me. It was my doing almost as much as it was the emperor's.

I knew it was him without needing to ask the question. I knew what he'd done, and I knew he had done it before and would do it again.

He'd seen something that wasn't his. Something beautiful and pure and loved beyond any emotion he knew, and he had wanted it. She'd denied him in front of the entire court, embarrassed him and dented his ego. So he'd snatched her, and beaten her, and taken what he had been refused before wrapping his hands around her neck and stealing her from this world once and for all.

The Fae couldn't tell lies. But secrets were easily kept by the dead.

I took Aalia's hand in mine one last time, the coldness of her touch so alien that it didn't even feel like it was her I was holding.

*You killed her.*

"And I'll avenge her," I swore in reply to my own mind. It wouldn't fix it. But it would at least reset the balance.

I pressed a kiss to the back of my sister's hand and stood, feeling the night pressing in on me as I forced myself to release her and turn away.

I was ice. A statue given breath. Inside, I was broken, but on the outside, a calm had consumed me entirely. A plan had formed within my mind, and I would see it done no matter the cost it bore.

I strode from the temple and into the night, the cicadas calling to the moon all around me as I turned toward the river and began walking.

The temple of Herdat sat alone on an outcrop at the bend in the river, right before it widened and swept out towards the distant sea. Death liked solitude after all, and though the temple had Fae visiting it daily, the walk from the city to its black stone walls was a long one. The thought was that the journey brought you closer to the dead, finding memories and ghosts in the solitude as you travelled the well-worn cobbles towards the iron door of the goddess of death.

I hadn't touched the door as I'd left, but many did, allowing the power to be drained from them as they stood there in sacrifice to Herdat and in honour of those they'd lost.

Death wasn't a common companion to the Fae, and with the length of our lives, it was always a tragedy. The murder of a lady of the court had brought many out of their homes to mourn. I hadn't recognised half of them and didn't care much for the rest. Their condolences had been empty, their sorrow inconsequential. None dared speak of what had happened or who might have done it. No one wished to utter the truth we all knew so blatantly.

Aalia had scorned the emperor and had died for it.

I focused on the sound of rushing water as I traversed the darkness towards the river's edge.

They were there already, the boat loaded with all the coin we'd been able to take from the family coffers, every valuable item which could be transported with ease. The twins were curled up tight against their grandparents, their tears fallen to exhaustion and sleep keeping hold of them for at least a little while.

I nodded to Aren's family but stopped dead at the edge of the small jetty.

"Come, Kyra," Aren said in a voice raw with grief, his bloodshot eyes illuminated by the dim light of the moon as he offered me his hand.

I didn't take it. Didn't move at all.

"We need to get into the straights before the sun comes up," Aren went on as if he couldn't tell what I was going to say, as if he hadn't already considered doing the exact same thing that I planned to a thousand times. "If we can get that far down river, then no one from the city will spy us. We'll have a better chance of escaping this place without-"

"Tell them I wanted a lifetime under the sky with them," I said slowly, my eyes on the twins as my chest tightened and my resolve threatened to crack for the first time. "Tell them I loved them more than words could ever convey. And tell them…not to wait to begin their adventures. I wasted my life looking at the horizon and never chasing it. The world was out there this entire time, and I never got to taste it."

"Kyra," Aren rasped, taking my hand by force and gripping it tightly. "Aalia wouldn't want this. She would never wish for you to lose your life in some impossible attempt at revenge for-"

"I'll see him dead, Aren," I swore, taking a gilded knife from my pocket and pulling the sheath from it to reveal the iron blade. We'd had this discussion already, both of us desperate to fulfil the task, though the impossibility of it had convinced Aren out of the idea in the end, especially when I'd made him think about the twins. They deserved better than to lose both parents. But me? I was expendable. He just hadn't wanted to admit it until now. "I'll see him bleeding and sobbing at my feet for taking her from us."

Aren's throat bobbed with the desire to see that too, his fist closing and then opening as he looked over his shoulder to the sleeping twins in his parents' arms.

"You'll never get close enough to do it," he breathed, the weight of his words falling over me because he believed they were true enough to have spoken them aloud.

"I will," I told him just as firmly, letting him see my truth too. "I plan on making whatever deals I need to, with whichever gods I have to, to see it done. She was my joy, Aren. I won't attempt any kind of life without her in it. Especially not while that piece of shit still draws breath."

Aren frowned as his grip on my hand tightened, words forming on his lips before falling away again as he saw my decision on this. I wouldn't be swayed. I wouldn't be turned.

"You'll come find us when it's done," he said firmly, and I managed a smile, a bittersweet smile for that pretty wish. We both knew there would be no surviving this for me. If by some miracle I ended the life of the emperor, I would never escape his guards.

"I'll see you in the Garden one day if not," I swore to him. "Aalia and I will wait for you there on a swing seat just like the one beyond the river by the house."

His eyes roamed between mine, and I knew he was picturing her there now, her bare toes in the long grass, a sweet smile on her lips as she beckoned us over. She was at peace, waiting for us in the fullness of the flowers, a summer breeze in the air.

A tear tracked down his cheek and I raised my hand to brush it aside. "Live well for their sake," I whispered. "Find that adventure, love fiercely, die bravely. We'll meet again, brother."

Aren choked back a sob as he drew me into his arms, my face pressing to his chest, and I returned his embrace knowing that this was it. I would never see them again. The family my sweet sister had gifted me, drifting away downriver in search of a new land and a new life. They would change their names when they arrived in Souvion. They would use their wealth to establish themselves and never speak of their past. And if by any chance, the queen of Souvion ever discovered who they were and why they had come to seek refuge in her kingdom, I was confident she would protect them. She was one of the few Fae queens who had never been afraid of Farish. She opposed him openly, even if it had never quite come to war, and would welcome them into her court should the truth present itself. But I hoped it never did. I hoped they could simply avoid the question of when and where they'd come from and focus entirely on where they were going. An adventure primed just for them. A new life where perhaps they could find happiness again, despite all they'd had so cruelly stolen from them.

We parted in silence, no goodbyes escaping us while Aren moved to sit with his children, drawing them into his arms as the boat set out towards the distant sea.

I remained standing there, immobile, my gaze fixed on the silver hair of the twins who I loved more than life itself as they headed away from me for the final time.

I watched until the horizon swallowed them and the boat was lost beyond it, their path set, just as mine was.

*Your fault,* the voice inside me screamed, and I accepted the lashings of her words. She was me and yet she wasn't. I was nothing but this cold vessel for vengeance now. Who knew what I might become once I achieved it?

I turned my back on the river, feeling so cold that I could have sworn frost marked my footsteps in my wake.

I could feel the eyes of the gods on me. They knew as well as I did that I intended to keep my word on this. The death of an emperor meant nothing to me in the wake of my sister.

I hadn't lied to Aren. I was willing to make a deal with any god to see this done. But I didn't need just *any* god. There were two who claimed the crowns as the most powerful of their kind. Saresh, keeper of the sun and giver of life.

I had already begged him for anything he might wish for to return my sister to me, but he hadn't so much as replied to my call. He had heard it all before, no doubt, the desperate pleas of those left behind to the one god known to breathe life into the world, but he had never answered anyone before me, and he ignored me just as surely.

So that left an option which none but the most desperate would attempt to bargain with.

Herdat. Goddess of death and ruin, gatekeeper to the Garden, master of souls.

I stepped back into her temple, my heart falling still as I spied the empty altar, the priests and priestesses having taken Aalia's body in my absence. They were somewhere in the depths of this place now, preparing her for burial. Speaking the rites over her body to help her stick to her path during her final walk into the Garden.

*You did this. You killed her. You should have done more, should have taken her place. You never should have let her walk out that morning.*

I closed my eyes to ward off the vision of that empty altar, but the words which were screamed from within myself only grew louder.

I turned back to the iron door, reaching for it blindly before pushing it shut, my palms flat to the hateful metal as I suppressed a groan at the nausea which rolled through me from the contact. My knees buckled as I felt my energy waning, my Affinities dwindling within me and my spine tingling as even the ghost of my wings seemed to wither away. I hadn't flown since I'd lost her. Likely wouldn't ever fly again.

"Herdat," I ground out as my knees collided with the hard stone and my body quaked from the prolonged contact with the iron. "I beg you for the power I will need to gain entry to the palace to seek vengeance for my sister."

Several seconds passed as I trembled there, the vile spell the iron had laid on me weakening me to my very core, but I simply called out to her again. And again.

The fifth time I called her name, the air shivered in reply and a scream caught in the back of my throat as something twisted in the shadows at my back.

I gasped as I turned from the door the same moment the torches which had been burning around the circular temple all guttered out.

Death lurked in the spaces between the shadows, its call a sweet caress on the air as Herdat shifted closer in the darkness.

*"And what might I get in payment for such a boon?"* a voice of nightmares purred in my ear, every muscle in my body tightening as the desire to wet myself and run screaming from this place nearly consumed me.

I bit into my cheek so hard that I drew blood, focusing on the memory of my sister's body, murdered for the crime of refusing the emperor's demands.

"I know you relish blood and suffering," I whispered, taking my dagger and unsheathing it before slicing a deep gash into my own arm.

I cried out at the pain of it as I struck the vein, my blood spraying hot and fast against the wall. Herdat moaned in feminine appreciation as my skin began knitting itself back together again, my Affinities healing the wound over in a matter of moments.

*"Oh, what fun we could have, daughter of Luciet. How I could watch you suffer and bleed for me without end while her power maintains you."*

A strike of sharp claws collided with my shoulder, and I was knocked to the floor as my blood spilled again, a yell of pain echoing from the walls which made Herdat's power pulse all around me.

"Is that your price?" I panted, willing to pay it if that was what this took, but it seemed too simple, too easy. The priests and priestesses who dedicated their lives to the worship of Herdat offered her as much pain and suffering as they could endure on a daily basis. I'd never understood the appeal personally, but there were plenty of them who did so, and other Fae often came from the city to offer up their pain in worship of her too, so it didn't seem like something she would be short on.

*"No,"* Herdat breathed in my ear, and I flinched as I pushed myself to my feet once more, turning wildly in the dark as I sought her out. *"I will give you what you need to gain entry to the palace, young soul. All I ask in return is that you spill as much of his blood as you can. Make it hurt, pretty thing. Make him scream and suffer for me. I have waited so very long to taste his end."*

My lips parted, then closed, my answer so simple that it seemed impossible.

"I want nothing more than to make him suffer," I snarled, straightening my spine as I felt the sinful presence of the goddess circling me. "That won't be a problem."

Herdat inhaled so deeply that she drew the breath from inside my own lungs, a soft moan escaping her as she feasted on that truth.

*"Oh, pretty little thing. You will enjoy his death so very much. I do believe you could become something far greater than you are once you have a taste for it. Once you see what joy his punishment serves you."*

I swallowed a lump in my throat, wondering if there could be any truth to her words. I had never killed before, but I had no doubt in my mind that I could do this. I wouldn't flinch, and she was right – if I pulled it off, then I was almost certain I would find enjoyment in it too.

The screaming of the little lost girl inside of me quieted at that thought, and I wondered if she feared me. If I feared myself and what the death of my sweet Aalia had created in me. But it was far too late for all of that, and I knew it.

"What will you give me?" I asked, unsure what I would even need to accomplish such a task, and Herdat's sultry laughter filled the space before she replied.

*"You shall have the power to speak the words you need to gain entry to his palace. They shall fall from your lips like drops of dew, set to sow the seeds of a new world for your kind and mine alike."*

"That's it?" I whispered, uncertain of what she even meant by that.

*"That's it. But be warned, sweet soul, that if you do this, the gods themselves*

*will riot. The world may crack and tear in two. Chaos shall rise and the dawn will break upon a new and different hour. This is your last chance to avoid corruption. Turn from this path or follow it with your whole heart. The power is yours."*

The oppressive weight lifted from the room, and I stumbled backwards as I felt her departing, her words ringing in the air like a curse of their own, but I didn't understand their meaning.

It didn't matter anyway. I would pay whatever price necessary to see my sister's killer dead, and damn the consequences.

## CHAPTER EIGHT

I walked towards the palace with my heart thumping to a steady rhythm and my breathing slow.

A calm had fallen over me the moment I'd set out for this place.

I hadn't said goodbye to anyone. I had no more room left in my heart for words of condolence and grief, and I couldn't tell them goodbye honestly anyway. I had some friends I would miss, and I hoped Imra and the others would continue to run the clinics without me, but this was not a task I could turn from.

Revenge wasn't something I had indulged in often, but I couldn't let this moment pass. I couldn't allow that wretch of a man to keep his throne and his life after disregarding hers so easily.

My sister had been beautiful in all the ways that actually mattered, but he had only cared about the way she looked and how he wanted to use that beauty for his own desires, to bend and break it, destroy and devour it.

The pale blue dress I wore hugged my figure and skimmed against my thighs, the movement of the fabric revealing the curve of my breasts and flashes of my legs as I strode toward the royal palace, walking straight between the still pools where I knew beasts to reside. No fear touched me. Death was the least of my concerns now, my one and only duty the sole focus of my thoughts.

The guards watched me approach, one of them glancing to the sky as if noting the late hour, but none of them said a word until I was standing right before them.

"What's your business here?" the most senior among the four asked, his gaze slipping over my body before returning to my face.

No recognition coloured his features nor any of the others, and though I wasn't surprised – the royal court was huge and I attended as infrequently as possible – I was relieved.

My lips parted on the words I needed to utter to gain entry to this place, but I stalled, feeling the weight of many eyes suddenly upon me and glancing over my shoulder as if I might spot the gods all crowded close, eager to find out what I might do.

"It's a beautiful night," I muttered, buying myself time as my pulse picked up a notch, the reality of what I intended sinking into me. Fae couldn't speak an untruth. It wasn't possible. And yet Herdat had offered me the gift of the words I would need to gain entry, so I had to assume that was what she meant. The power to deceive with the words I spoke.

"It is," the guard agreed, his eyes not moving from me. "And you should tell us what brings you out in it at such a late hour."

Whispers began at my back and my skin prickled with apprehension, my mouth drying out at the thought of speaking a lie.

It couldn't be done. There was no way. And if the weight of the air all around me was anything to go by, the gods didn't want me to attempt it either.

But as I considered my options, weighed this choice and what the alternative would require, I lifted my chin.

My sister was dead. There was nothing in this world or the next which could be stolen from me now, so either this would work, or it wouldn't. Either way, I had come here with the intention of killing the man responsible for the end of my truest love, and I wouldn't be turning back.

I felt a brush of ruinous fingers across my lips, a breath of sin in my ear and a weight of darkness settling on my soul as I solidified the decision within myself.

Herdat had felt it. She knew. And she had unleashed the seal on my lips, allowing me to speak as I willed, truth or lie, honesty or falsehood.

It had never been done. The gods had forged us in their idea of perfection, creating creatures of purity with the gifts of their own blessings. There had long been whispers of our corruption, of how in the millennia which had passed since our creation, the Fae had begun to rebel against the controls put on our existence, the price set for our immortality. We had rebelled in small ways, evading answers instead of speaking plainly, keeping secrets and committing sins. Skills intended for the protection of our kind had been turned into weapons of war. Affinities for seduction and beauty had been twisted into tools of manipulation. Games were played, rules broken, laws changed. We weren't the creatures we had been when we were created, and I had heard more than a few murmurings of the gods' discontent on that fact.

They had never intended for us to seek out the darkness in this world, but with each act of immorality, wickedness, and depravity, we fell from grace.

Once, our kind never could have contemplated the act I was about to commit, but here I was, ready to break one of the cardinal laws of our race.

Fae cannot lie.

"The emperor has need of me," I said simply, the words rolling from my tongue like a sip of finest wine, their poison tasting so sweet that none of them even noticed it as they swallowed. "He asked for me to join him in his bed chamber."

Silence echoed in the space that followed my lie. An implosion of all things which we had been and might have become. It was like every god in existence sucked in a sharp breath and the world was robbed of oxygen for it.

My lungs stilled in my chest and a deep purr seemed to echo from the centre of the universe itself as Herdat's power swelled around me.

Carioth was laughing and Saresh was bellowing my name as if it were a curse, while Luciet began to scream and scream and-

I blinked and a veil seemed to lift from my eyes. One which stole the knowledge of the gods and their reactions from me, leaving me standing there, staring blankly at the four guards. They gazed at me in expectation, seeming not to have noticed the cataclysmic change which had taken place in the fabric of reality itself.

"Sorry," I murmured. "Did you say something?"

"I…asked if you know the way?" a tall guard near the back repeated, and I realised he had already spoken the words once. No questions beyond that, no suspicion, or accusations. I had told them a lie and they had no reason at all to doubt me. Fae *couldn't* lie, so I had to be telling the truth. It was incredibly simple and utterly terrifying.

"Oh, no, I don't." I admitted, and the corner of his mouth twitched with amusement, his gaze moving down my body briefly before landing back on my face.

"You excited?" he teased, and I had to fight the inclination to sneer at the idea of truly bedding the emperor. I would though. I had realised that when I'd set out on this plan. If I reached his chambers to find him awake, and I couldn't easily strike, then I would do whatever I had to. If that meant bedding him before I killed him, then I could endure it. Though the mere thought of it had me wanting to scream and scream until my throat ripped itself raw.

"I am," I agreed, letting them think what they wanted of that. I *was* excited though – excited to drive my blade into the black heart of the beast who had hurt my Aalia.

"Come. I'll show you the way." The guard jerked his chin, then set off into the palace, and I ignored the looks I gained from the others as I followed him.

We walked in silence, passing into the deeper parts of the palace which I had never so much as glimpsed on my few visits to this place in the past.

I chewed on my bottom lip as I followed him, wondering if Aalia had seen these same corridors when she was brought here. Had she walked down them willingly or been dragged by force? Had she fought this fate or accepted it, thinking he would get what he wanted then let her go? Or had she been smuggled in through some secret entrance? Brought in like the ugly secret she was always intended to be.

He'd killed her to hide the truth, and surely he wouldn't have allowed many witnesses to his crimes? But I doubted the emperor had taken her body out into the city and dumped it himself. So at least some of the guards in this place had to be complicit in his atrocities. I wondered if the male I was following was one of them. Maybe he'd helped cover it up or had hidden other horrors in this pretty palace of corruption.

I didn't know.

But all I did know was that Farish's eternal reign would come to an end at my hands, or I would give my life in the attempt to end it. No more would this tyrant play god with the lives of his subjects.

We headed up a narrow stairway, Herdat echoing my steps, the touch of her darkness within me somehow letting me know that we were going the right way. We passed several more guards who ignored me entirely before I was led into a huge private living area. The candles had burned down low and no servants lingered inside, but I could see two heavy doors beyond the richly furnished sitting room.

"The emperor's bed chamber is on the right," the guard informed me, a taunting smirk on his lips. "No doubt he is eagerly awaiting you."

"It will be one of the most memorable nights of his life," I agreed, my gaze remaining locked on that closed door as the guard backed away and shut me inside.

I released a slow breath, counting to one hundred to be certain the guard had gone, his footsteps receding beyond the door, then I slowly pulled the dagger from the sheath hidden in the folds of my dress.

I took a step forward, then another, the feeling of the gods' eyes on me present once more, though I felt Herdat closest of all, her dark power disturbing the embers in the fire as I passed it, making them swirl out before me like a herald announcing Farish's fate.

The voice inside my head had been notably silent throughout this, but I felt the attention of that fractured part of me fixed on my actions now, like she was watching, cheering me on, wanting this too. The pieces of me reunited in this most powerful need for revenge.

My fingers burned with some untold power as I silently turned the doorknob, letting myself into the extravagant bedroom, the four-poster bed sitting proudly at its centre.

A fire burned in there too, the flames flickering rapidly as they felt the touch of darkness creeping close.

*"Pay me in the blood of an emperor,"* Herdat's hungry purr rattled through my head, but I pushed her out, not wanting her needs and desires to cloud my own. His death was mine alone. Let her feast on his pain and his blood, but I would be the maker of his demise in its entirety.

The knife warmed in my hand, the metal humming with an anticipation of its own. I stepped across the tiled floor quietly, relishing this moment before the end of him, where he was at my mercy and knew nothing at all of his oncoming death.

My heart was racing now, thundering to its own beat as a darkness filled me in a way I had never known before. I hadn't ever experienced hatred like this, nor craved retribution or vengeance in the way I did now as I stood over his sleeping form, the knife gripped tight in my fist.

I inhaled deeply, savouring his last moment on this earth, then I struck like a viper from a pit.

The dagger slammed through flesh and bone as it pierced his back, the force it required far more than I had anticipated. My knees hit the bed as I ripped it free again to the glorious chorus of the scream which sprung from his lips.

Farish lurched away from me, but I was faster, lunging after him and striking again, the blade catching on his ribs as I slammed it into him, and I wrapped my free hand around the hilt too so that I could use the fullness of my strength.

He choked on his own blood, screaming again, and oh how beautiful that sound was, how fucking blissful and freeing.

A noise of utter ecstasy escaped me as the power over life and death consumed me, and I raised myself up above him, tearing the blade free once more. An arc of blood sprayed across the room, coating my dress and skin with its hot splatter, and I grinned like a demon who had just been anointed in sin.

Farish threw an arm out towards me, bellowing for his guards while I countered the blow with a slash from my blade, spilling more blood onto the pure white sheets and embracing the darkness as it swept in to fill the holes which had been torn through my soul in the moment of my sweet sister's death.

"Do you know me?" I cooed as I shoved him down onto his back thrust the dagger into his chest.

I looked right into his eyes as he screamed again, this pitiful, desperate noise from a man who claimed to be so much more than those he ruled over. Where was the eternal emperor now? Where was his unquestioned power and the loyalty of his dear subjects?

"Do you know my sister?" I hissed the more poignant question, snatching the blade free before stabbing, stabbing, stabbing.

This fury in me had no beginning and no end. The bloodlust could never be matched nor sated, and yet I wanted all I could claim of it.

I didn't care what that made me. What he'd made me. Because I had come to collect this debt, and I would relish every god-sworn moment of it.

Farish bucked beneath me, and I moved to straddle him as I slashed at the arm which tried to throw me from him.

He was striking me, his fists pounding against my skin, but I could hardly even feel it. His desperation to live on was nothing to my ruinous desire to annihilate him, and my knife sank into his flesh over and over and over. I cracked right down to the centre of my being, and I began to grin like a wolf with a fawn between its paws.

"Aalia was worth a million of you," I spat, stabbing again, blood flying, screams ringing. "She was all that you could never hope to be. So much better than all of us. And you should have left her alone."

I could feel Herdat standing in my shadow, the cold whisper of her breath on the back of my neck as she watched and relished in this act. Her power slipped into me wherever it could, this obsidian darkness which stained me from the inside out, coaxing laughter to pour from my throat, a wilder smile to spread across my face.

His screams were perfection in their desperate, pathetic need for salvation which wasn't coming. The guards were likely sprinting for us right now, but I was already dressed from head to toe in his blood, the sheets-stained scarlet with it, and there would be no bringing him back from this.

As if that thought had reminded me of what I was, my Affinities flared within me, the healing magic which coursed through my veins throbbing like a reminder of what I had been born to do. I could likely save him. Even now, as he lay beneath me, his screams fading and his thrashing growing oh-so-weak, I might have been able to draw him back to me if I were to use those gifts the way I had always done before.

But I wouldn't use them. Probably not ever again. Let him suffer and die at my hand. Let him fucking beg. And he *was* begging, sobbing and snivelling through the blood, pleading for his pathetic life as I leaned down and drops of red fell from the tendrils of my dark hair.

"Admit what you did," I whispered, the dagger lodged in his chest, likely puncturing his heart. "Tell me what you did to Aalia."

"I killed her," he choked out, blood spraying from his lips to coat mine as I leaned in so close I might have been going to kiss him. I licked the drops of it away, tasting his death on my tongue and relishing the sweetness of it.

"I admit it," he gasped. "I'm…s-sorry. Please, just stop. Stop-"

"Stop, stop, stop," I mocked, footsteps pounding through the room beyond his bed chamber, guards so close and yet too far. "Did she beg too? Did she beg you to let her return to her family? To her twins and her husband? To me?"

"Yes," he panted, and I sneered down at him, letting him see exactly what kind of monstrous creature he had created in me with her death. "I'm sorry. I'm so-"

"Let Herdat burn you," I cursed him. "Let her feast on your rotten soul until it is corrupted beyond recognition. Let peace never find you. And let you remain lost beyond the gates of the Garden for all of time, lingering in madness and chaos."

I ripped the blade from his chest just as the door was flung open behind me, swiping it across his throat with a blow so savage that it half decapitated him.

Herdat moaned with pleasure as his death swept through the room like a wave of pure energy, right into her destructive grasp. I fell back onto my knees, laughing wildly with the empty triumph of his demise.

The guards were yelling and screaming in panic, grabbing me and tearing me off of the bed, my dagger lost among the bloodied sheets and left there with his corpse while I praised the gods for aiding me and laughed that hollow, endless laugh.

I didn't fight them, barely even noticed them as the reality of my victory sank into my bones and I was left with the gaping hole of nothingness where all I'd once loved and lived for had been.

"Take me," I implored Herdat, her power billowing around me as she drank in the death I had offered her and feasted on every scrap of it.

I saw her then, her horrifying form emerging from the shadows in the corner of the room, the candles guttering the moment my gaze met with her terrifying presence, the guards all shrieking in alarm as they were left blind in the dark.

Her clawed hand found my jaw and she lifted it, the lips of the goddess brushing with mine as she spoke straight into my mind.

*"Ask me for more and it shall be granted."*

Light blazed before my eyes and a vision shuttered into me, one where I accepted her offer and allowed her power to flood through me in its entirety. She showed me the eternal throne where Farish had built his kingdom, except instead of the tyrant king sitting upon it, I was there, dressed in blood with a crown of bones on my brow.

My eyes were dark and empty, a cruel smile lifting my lips as I looked over my empire, my riches, the Fae all set to serve me however I pleased. The path to that throne was nothing but ash and bone, death and carnage, but she showed me how I would delight in it. How I would be set free from my grief if only I accepted her offer.

My body was humming with the thrill of the death I had just dealt out, and the ache in my soul was desperate for reprieve, for the grief to be gone.

*"It will all be ours. Say yes and bring about the Age of Ruin. Say yes and set yourself free."*

Power rose within me as I considered it, this dark, tempestuous sea of destruction which could be mine so easily. With that one word. Yes.

But as my lips parted on that answer, as I let myself consider an eternity of power and freedom from the pain in my heart, I heard that screaming girl again. The me who wasn't quite me. She didn't want to be free of the pain, she didn't want to forget. And as I forced my thoughts onto my sister, I saw her there, standing in the Garden, smiling at me softly, her hand reaching out as if to touch me.

She was all I wanted. Not a life of riches and power, or darkness and fury. Her. The girl who was so lost to me that all I really wanted was to join her in death.

"No," I said simply. Easily. Because it *was* easy to choose death in that moment. Where I could see her waiting for me beyond the confines of this world. I had seized the justice she deserved and that was the only wish I had remaining for myself here. So let death take me. Let it take me to her.

Herdat snapped towards me with a defiant snarl, but a deep power resonated through the air and my eyes widened as Luciet burst into being before me, her skin coated in leaves and flowers, the goddess of healing. She cast an energy which seared my flesh before the two of them exploded in a blast of power which hurled me back against the wall.

I hit it hard, the guards surrounding me thrown away too, none of them rising from where they fell.

I pushed to my hands and knees, blinking at the destruction of the room, the furniture blasted apart and the dead emperor laying amid a coffin of bloodstained sheets.

*"Run,"* Luciet hissed in my ear, and I did.

I wasn't running for my life, so I didn't know what I ran for, but my feet hit the floor step after step, and I ripped the door open before charging down a staircase.

Bells were ringing all over the palace, the sound of booted feet colliding with the tiles as guards charged back and forth, hollering orders and hunting the palace for whoever had attacked the emperor.

*Me.*

They were hunting me like grouse in the long grass, and the power of the gods was the only thing which propelled me onwards through this hopeless maze of stone corridors and lavish extravagance.

It was so dark in the palace, every torch and fire guttered out as if a magical breeze had snuffed them all out at once, and I had to think Karu, the bird god of wind and storms, might be responsible for it.

The world was shifting around me, something changing in the fabric of all I knew, and I felt somehow responsible for it, for the way the gods were riled up, the way they hissed and spat and fought, whispering all around me.

Something was wrong. Inherently wrong with the world as a whole, and I was standing in the centre of the storm as it erupted.

## CHAPTER NINE

I launched myself around a corner and barely stifled a scream as strong arms caught me, a man almost twice my size whirling me in his grip before pushing me back against the closest wall.

"Kyra?" Calvari gasped in surprise, his features lost in the darkness, but I recognised his voice as his shadow loomed over me.

"What are you doing here?" I asked him, trying to pull free, but his hold on my arm remained tight.

"I had a feeling you might have come here," he grunted. "When I went to your house and found it abandoned."

The clouds shifted beyond the window beside us, pale moonlight filtering in and throwing his features into a little focus at last. He was frowning, concern and something I couldn't place in his dark eyes as he frowned down at me in the shadows, still not seeing me clearly, still unaware of the blood which marked my flesh in evidence of what I'd done. And I realised then that he knew, he knew who had killed Aalia, and he knew I would come here, so he had come too. But I just didn't know why.

"You know what he did?" I breathed, looking up into the eyes of the man I had spent countless nights with. The man who had shared my bed and been to my home often enough to know my sister, to have eaten at her table and seen her playing with her children. He'd experienced the kindness of her soul first hand. He knew her, and yet his fingers were biting into my arm, his grip on me unrelenting like he was afraid I might try and escape.

"I'm sworn into the service of the emperor," he replied, something flashing through his eyes which could have been sorrow, or regret, but he wasn't letting go, and a sour feeling pooled in my gut as I took in his stance before me. "My duty is to him."

"And what if he was dead?" I breathed, the hint of a smile forming on my lips as I looked up at him in the brightening light as the moon broke free of the clouds outside, parting the shadows around me and he finally took in the blood that coated me, reading the truth of what I'd done all too clearly.

The shouts of the royal guards filled the air, and I knew they would be upon us at any moment. They would capture me and kill me and oh…how I welcomed the prospect of death. Let Herdat take my stained soul and deliver it to the Garden where my sister waited for me.

"Then my duty would fall to his heir, Savinia. I am bound in service to the royal line, and whoever killed him would be a traitor to the crown," Calvari said, his fingers still biting into my skin as he stared down at me like he was trying to make it false. Like he wanted to will the blood from my flesh and the murderous glee from my golden eyes. But he knew. And he understood it too, because if he was any kind of Fae, then he would have done the same in my place.

"You would serve a man who killed my sister for the simple denial of his attention? You think a brutal beast who takes what is not given freely and destroys a mother, a sister, a gentle, beautiful soul for pure spite and embarrassment is worthy of your devotion?" I hissed, the thundering footsteps drawing closer still. It was over. I'd known that the moment I walked into this place, and all I really felt at that fact was relief.

Calvari frowned for a moment, like he really might have been questioning that undying loyalty, like some part of him knew how fucked up it was to blindly follow the rule of a Fae who would do the things Farish had done. But then a guard somewhere deeper into the palace shouted out in his hunt for me, and it was like a switch flipped in the depths of Calvari's gaze.

"Sometimes, when I was fighting for my life and my empire on the battlefield, I would think of you, Kyra. I would wonder if I might love you one day. If I might take you for my bride if we ever got the time to see if what we had might be more. But I see now why that never came to pass. You're wild, impulsive, and dangerous. You forget that the strength of the empire is the strength of us all, and that the emperor is the divinely anointed head of our fates."

His words were filling my veins with that ice again, the truth of who he was and what he believed settling over me like a wet cloud. Disappointment and something akin to hurt twisted in my chest, but more than that, there was something far worse, because he was still talking instead of handing me over, still speaking even though there was no reason to, and with every word that passed his lips, the tension in my limbs grew like I already knew what he was going to say, even though I stood before him utterly ignorant of every word.

My muscles tensed where he held me, the power of my Affinities rising to the surface of my skin as I called on them to aid me, filling my flesh with the power Bentos had gifted me while I let Calvari speak.

"It is our duty to serve the emperor in whatever way he sees fit. If your sister had simply bowed to his desire, then she would still be…" He blew out a harsh breath and I recognised that look for what it was – guilt.

"You met her in the market," I stated, and Calvari flinched the barest amount, but he didn't deny it. "The emperor had seen you with me, so he asked his Fated Warrior to prove his loyalty by delivering Aalia to his bed."

"Kyra," Calvari breathed, his grip bruising while his gaze punctured mine, like he wanted to beg for my understanding but was struggling for the words.

"She trusted you because of me," I went on, the truth becoming so clear now. "Did Carioth tell the emperor of the trick he had played with our memories, or did that simply make your job even easier?"

Calvari swallowed thickly before continuing, his words a rush, like he was a desperate man seeking absolution. "The emperor believed the gods were playing games. I don't know precisely what he had discerned from his advisors and the priests and priestesses, but he was confident she would be in the market. Kyra, you have to understand. It was a test of my loyalty. I had no choice-"

"No choice but to save your own sorry arse," I bit back, and he recoiled from the lash of the words as if I'd struck him.

"I didn't know he'd kill her," Calvari insisted, shaking me with his desperation to make me understand. But I understood all too well. He had tracked her down, used her trust in him and brought her to the bed of a man he knew she had no interest in fucking. So what if he'd believed Farish would release her once he'd taken what he wanted? That didn't make it any better.

I should have suspected him from the start. He had been entirely absent since Aalia's death, no doubt caught up in self-pity and guilt, but I didn't give a fuck about how he felt. Because he had been the one to bring her here, he had been willing to let her suffer for however long Farish had desired purely to save his own pathetic soul.

Rage consumed me, and beneath the rage was something so much worse. Betrayal.

He was supposed to have just been a man I fucked when the fates aligned to put us in each other's paths, but that had been the arrangement we'd made over a decade ago. In that time, we had shared a friendship along with our bodies, perhaps I had even been fool enough to believe it might have been something more than that from time to time. We had been something to one another. He had been welcomed into my home, he had dined with my sister, laughed with her husband, smiled at her children, and then…this.

"When he summoned me to dispose of her body, something broke in me, Kyra," Calvari went on, his words a lashing sea against the walls of my mind as a heavy ringing started in my ears.

He was still talking but I couldn't hear him, my entire being consumed with the knowledge of what he'd done and my flesh buzzing with the weight of my Affinities as I called out to Bentos to aid me.

I felt the brush of a kiss against my cheek, and I knew the god was answering my prayers.

I pushed up onto my toes and kissed Calvari, cutting off his words, the heat of his mouth against my bloodstained lips awakening a feral beast within me.

I'd once thought I knew this man. It had never been close to love, but it had been something, or the prospect of something. A kindred spirit, a taste of the adventure I'd once longed for so hopelessly. But I could see now that the freedom I'd seen in him had only ever been an imagined one. He wasn't free. He hadn't been living some fabled life of adventure and excitement. He was a coward who bowed to the whims of a monster. And he was going to pay for letting that blind devotion steal my beautiful sister from this world.

Bentos' power imbued my flesh as I pushed into the Affinities the god of seduction had gifted me, and Calvari groaned as he drew my body flush to his, lust colouring his actions as his lips parted for my tongue and my hand ran down his abs towards his belt.

For several seconds he was blinded by his desire for me, his cock hardening against my stomach just as my fingers found the knife strapped to his hip.

"She's here!" a voice bellowed behind him, and Calvari jerked back a second before I thrust his own blade into his neck, the iron sinking deep and cutting fatally.

I sneered as I backed away from him, a feral, animal glare which was as hollow as my soul and as empty as my heart.

Calvari dropped to his knees before me, clutching at the blade where it still protruded from his neck, staring at me in shock and horror while two guards grabbed me from behind.

My healing Affinities awoke as I watched him gasping for breath like a fish out of water and I let the light of that power glimmer in my fingertips as I was dragged away.

"I could save you," I called. "I could heal you in a matter of moments, all praise to Luciet. "I could make you whole again, Calvari. Perhaps if the emperor were to demand it, I would be a faithful subject and bow to his desire to do so. Oh…but he's dead now too, isn't he? Perhaps when you meet him in the Garden, you can ask what his command would have been. Would he have ordered me to heal you? Or would he have just told you to accept your fate the way you accepted Aalia's?"

Calvari choked and spluttered, blood spilling from his lips as the guards hauled me away from him, and I cursed that twisted tendril of betrayal which was carving its way into my heart, reminding me who had been responsible for allowing him into our lives.

I found some small sense of satisfaction at the sight of him falling to his face on the tiles which his precious emperor had kept so brightly polished, but it didn't bring her back.

*Your fault*, that voice inside me spat with venom, and I knew that she was right on that count.

"One kiss from the one who betrayed me!" I called loudly, the deal I'd made with the god of tricksters resounding through my mind as I realised what I had done, and I swear I heard Carioth chuckling in reply.

# CHAPTER TEN

I'd expected the guards to kill me. I hadn't cared. I'd gotten justice for my sister, and I had nothing left to live for without her anyway. Of course, fate had a much crueller destiny in mind for me in the end.

I shivered in the dank cavern where I'd been left to rot since the night I'd killed the emperor, his blood still staining my clothes and skin, the sound of his pleas still ringing in my ears.

I had thought it would feel better than this. I had thought that gaining this vengeance would have earned me at least a little solace. But it hadn't brought her back. It didn't change what he had done. My sister was still lost to this world, her children still left to cry themselves to sleep night after night, her husband left to raise them alone. And me? Well, I was just…left.

I thought of Aren and focused on him and the two beautiful little creations they had made together. I wondered if they were in Souvion yet, where the guards of our city held no jurisdiction and the queen who sat upon the throne there would be all too welcoming of someone who'd had a hand in the emperor's death. Though they would keep that secret to themselves if they could. If they were there, then they'd be safe. It was the one good thing in all of this.

All I had to do was keep the secret of their destination secret if I was interrogated, and I would embrace any and all forms of torture willingly before I ever spoke of their location.

I wondered if I could still lie. If that gift had been left with me or had only worked that once. If I could, then perhaps I could use that to my advantage, send the royal guards in the wrong direction altogether. Though I didn't dare speak aloud to test the theory.

The sick feeling which pressed at the base of my throat had become normal after days of being shackled in iron and left to starve down here in the dark.

I'd slept twice when exhaustion had forced me to keel over, the iron manacles cutting into my flesh as I hung from them, and even the bite of the cold, damp stone which surrounded me did nothing to keep me awake any longer. Not that I had gained anything in sleep. All I'd been gifted were the memories of my sister's cold hand in mine, of the discoloured bruises around her neck in death.

Water dripped in an endlessly changing rhythm somewhere close by, a small pool just out of sight around the bend. My feet were still damp from when they'd dragged me through it when they'd brought me down here days ago, the cold, wetness of this place making certain they couldn't dry. No doubt the skin within my silk shoes was suffering for it, but I hadn't been able to bring myself to try and remove them. I hadn't even tried to remove the iron shackles which were secured around my wrists.

The thin, once pale blue silk of the gown I'd worn when I'd snuck into the emperor's bed clung to my body and did nothing to help banish the cold from my limbs, the fabric near translucent now and stained with so much blood that you could hardly even tell what colour it had once been.

The sound of heavy footsteps approaching made me crack my eyes open, my head raising from where it had fallen to hang against my chest in the most comfortable position I could maintain while my arms were stretched out towards the walls either side of me.

"Has the heir decided what to do with her then?" a guard inquired, his voice familiar to me after days of hearing him and the others exchange words. They maintained a position guarding me out of sight, nearer the exit of the cavern beneath the palace where I was being held.

"Savinia has decided to allow me the honour of doling out punishment," a cold voice replied, letting me know what the emperor's daughter had decided should be done with me, the sound of his words seeming to slither across my ears, forcing a trickle of fear into me which I hadn't even realised I was capable of feeling anymore.

I knew who approached me. Kalir, the emperor's former advisor and Royal Prophet. He took the magic of the gods and wielded it like it was his own. Many spoke out against the things he and his kind practiced, but the emperor had always been too selfish to care for the fears of his people. He wasn't worried about angering the gods when he believed he had been blessed and favoured by them since his birth so very long ago.

I wondered if he still believed himself blessed now that he was lingering in the after. Who knew if he had found paradise or eternal torment, but I hoped with all that was left of me that it was the latter.

"Come to execute me?" I asked impassively, my voice a brittle thing as Kalir and the guard rounded the corner, the light of the torch the guard carried making my eyes prickle and sting after days left to linger in the dark.

"That would be all too simple an end for the Fae who killed our great emperor, would it not?" Kalir asked, the eerie brightness in his eyes making my skin pepper with goosebumps.

It wasn't natural what he was or what he took from the gods. I didn't care what justification his kind used; we shouldn't have wielded the power of our creators the way he did. Sorcery went far beyond the use of our Affinities.

The Royal Prophet was terrifying in his stature as well as his gifts. He was a huge man, both tall and broad, his head fully shaven and eyes two pits of nothing. I hated what he was and what he represented with his white robes which he never removed in public, the stark, bright colour a contrast to the deep stains I knew lined his rotten soul. Almost all of his power was taken through methods which weren't even whispered of, for all folk knew how twisted and depraved the Prophets were.

"I will die shortly either way," I muttered, not caring for their plans, only wanting one thing now. "And then I will finally be with my sister again in the Eternal Garden where nothing can touch me anymore."

"You think you will be welcomed into the Garden?" the guard scoffed, and I turned a cold look his way. "You're a murderer."

"I saved the kingdom from the rule of a tyrant. I stopped a monster from hurting anyone ever again. I believe I will be welcomed into the Garden for that," I assured him.

The back of Kalir's hand smacked across my face, throwing me to one side as I tasted blood and felt bone crack from the unnatural strength he held. My shoulder roared with agony as my weight was forced to hang from the shackle securing that arm, but I didn't let so much as a breath escape me, much less a cry of pain.

I rocked back around to face him, spitting my blood at his feet as the magic I had been gifted upon my birth sprung to life within me, my healing Affinity flaring as the power raced along my jaw and healed the wound. It was much harder than it should have been with the iron encasing my hands, but I came from a long line of powerful Fae, and even that beastly metal couldn't fully contain my magic.

Kalir's lips lifted in a savage grin as he watched my magic work, his overly bright eyes pinned to me as he nodded.

"She is perfect," he breathed, greed lighting his eyes.

"What do you intend to do with her?" the guard asked curiously, not like he cared or wanted to protect me, more like he was genuinely interested in what torture I was destined to endure.

"I will remake her," Kalir said, imbuing my limbs with fear as I wondered what he meant by that. There was no way he intended to offer me anything close to kindness or redemption, so I was certain any plans he had would only be designed to aid in my suffering. "I will bind her and create her in the image of a god itself."

"Why?" the guard asked as I frowned, not wanting anything at all other than death now.

"She is destined for power only ever known by the gods, but the price of it will be her will, her freedom, and her soul."

"What?" I breathed, my pulse picking up, though I didn't understand his words at all.

"You, the woman who disrespected the highest of all Fae in the most despicable of ways, will only ever know a life of servitude and submission from this day forth," Kalir said cruelly.

"You cannot break my will," I assured him, my jaw gritting with the knowledge that I would never bend to whatever he thought to force upon me. I would die first. And if not by their hands, then I would do so by my own.

"I won't give you the luxury of a choice."

Kalir jerked his chin at me before I could respond in any way and the guard moved forward, drawing a key from his pocket which he used to unlock the shackles which held me.

I let myself drop to my knees as I was released, the cold stone cutting into my skin and making me bleed once more, before my power rushed to fix it just as fast.

I feigned weakness, waiting for the guard to move behind me and haul me to my feet, while my attention fixed solely on the blade hanging from the sheath at his side.

I didn't intend to waste any time on whatever plans they had for punishing me. I was done with this world and all it had taken. I was done with this endless life. Because without Aalia in it, I was lost. She was the one constant I had held tight to, the one truth that had ever really counted for me. And now she was gone.

The guard heaved me up and I twisted sharply, slamming my fist into his jaw hard enough to knock him back, grasping the blade from his belt before turning it on myself. The steel brushed against the flesh between my breasts, and my muscles tensed as I moved to impale myself upon it. I only had to strike my heart and even my gifts couldn't save me.

But before I could go through with what I ached for so desperately, a strange and unholy power locked around my limbs, freezing them in place.

A gasp of fear escaped me as the guard lurched forward, ripping the blade from my frozen fingers before taking hold of me and squeezing my arm tightly. The power holding me fell away and I shuddered as I was whirled towards Kalir.

The Prophet was panting heavily, the dark skin of his bald head and brow speckled with beads of sweat, his gold embroidered robes dampened with it too. Whatever power he had just used to contain me was no Affinity I had ever known of. That was some twisted sorcery which he'd stolen from the lap of the gods themselves.

"I'm not letting you escape this fate, Esworn," he growled, the use of the cursed name stilling any words I held on my tongue. The Esworn were the worst of the Fae, those who had done atrocious things and had forfeited their right to even hold a name any longer. I wasn't like them. What I had done was no crime. "But I will make it easier on you if you give up the location of your brother-in-law and his children."

"I'll die before I give them up," I spat, and his eyes widened because he knew I spoke the truth. There was no lying for our kind. At least not so far as he knew. Which meant he really would make it easier on me if I spoke of their location too, but I meant what I said with every fibre of my being. I was already dead. If they wanted to cut me apart piece by piece before I met with death, then so be it. I had already faced the worst pain I could ever endure anyway in the loss of my sister, and no physical agony could be a match to that, nor enough to ever make me give up her remaining family.

"We'll see about that," Kalir muttered.

My heart began to race as I was hauled away from the cavern where I'd been held for days.

"Herdat, take me," I begged of the goddess, but I hadn't so much as imagined the presence of any of the gods close to me since I'd left that place of blood and death. She didn't answer me, didn't so much as acknowledge my request for death, and in the pit of my gut, I still felt that wrongness in the world which had begun with me speaking a lie. Something had changed with that act which she'd encouraged. The gods had been in uproar and now they were all too quiet.

We headed out into the brightness of the sun, the guard carrying me as the strength I'd managed to summon fled and I paid the price of days without nourishment while clad in iron.

I slumped against my captor, the ripe scent of him filling my nose as he carried me towards some unknown destination. I knew I should have been fighting harder. But it didn't really matter. Whatever was done to me now would still end the same way. I would find a way to end my life if they didn't do it for me. I would find a way to join her in death.

We strode away from the palace through the cool spring air, more guards surrounding us as we went and the sound of their booted feet on the ground carrying to me. The pastel shades of the blossoms blooming around us made my chest lighten, the trees swaying in a light breeze and the scent of spring caressing my senses, focusing on that instead of my destination.

We headed into the forest, following Kalir's directions until the light of the sky began to darken once again with the thickness of the canopy overhead.

We finally arrived in an open patch of woodland, the trees parting for it as if the hand of a god had swept the ground clear in this spot alone for some unknown purpose. Maybe even for this very moment.

In the centre of the space was a heavy wooden chair with an iron collar, the inside of it lined with sharpened spikes, locked to the top of it. There were carvings in the wood which made my skin prickle, effigies of the gods in their purest forms, the lines simple and yet endlessly intricate. It seemed as though every single god and goddess were represented in those carvings, each of them offered the same amount of space as a sign of respect to their power.

I began to fight as I was carried closer to that chair, the sight of the collar attached to it lighting fear in me beyond what I could even understand right now. I had never seen anything like it, but I could feel the power it held, sense the eyes of countless deities turning this way, and I knew in my soul that I wanted no part of this at all.

"Stop," I gasped as the guard's fingers bit into me, another coming to take hold of me too as they fought to contain me.

"Please," I begged, even though I knew it would do no good. I began to kick and fight, my nails catching and tearing on the metal of their armour as more hands gripped me and forced me to bend to their will.

Many hands pushed me down, their power overwhelming mine as I was shoved into the chair, forced to sit with my spine straight and my neck roughly strapped into the confines of the contraption at the top of it.

My head filled with the sound of a thousand whispers, their voices powerful and brimming with a range of emotions so potent that I could feel them rattling through my skin. The gods were all around me suddenly, some curious, some eager, others horrified or angry. It didn't seem to matter though; not one of them appeared to make their feelings known, and if the Fae surrounding me realised they were close, they paid no attention to their presence, instead focusing on me.

A scream escaped my lips just before the iron collar was locked into place around my throat. My breath stuck in my lungs as I felt a ring of sharpened points cutting into my neck from within the iron collar, and I stopped thrashing as the wounds forced the metal to make contact with my blood, every movement only driving them deeper into my skin though they weren't close enough to offer me the escape of death.

I tried to call on my healing power to aid me, but with the iron piercing my flesh there was nothing that it could do, and my stomach roiled from the taste of iron which coated my tongue.

"Tell us where your brother-in-law took his children," Kalir demanded calmly, as if he thought this would be enough to change my mind.

I spat at him, wincing from the movement as it made the iron spikes sink further into my flesh, but at least my point had been made clearly.

"I will never tell you," I hissed, my truth sizzling in the air and making itself known.

Kalir eyed me for several moments, then nodded, accepting that much and seeming to realise there wasn't a power on this earth that would break my resolve to keep this secret.

The guards disbanded and Kalir came to stand before me, taking a plain metal coin from his pocket and holding it up for me to see. It was big enough to fill the centre of his palm but completely smooth and unadorned, unlike any coin I'd ever seen. It wasn't currency, and the strange glow it emitted suggested it was so much more than a simple piece of precious metal.

"This coin shall be the master of your destiny from now until the end of time, Esworn," he purred, that unnatural light to his eyes burning more fiercely, and I could do nothing but stare up at him. "Prepare yourself," he added as he placed the coin on the ground before me and took a step back. "The power I am about to call upon will be anything but gentle with your cursed soul. But I can make it hurt less at any point – all you have to do is tell me where they are hiding and I will let you sleep throughout the process. Or keep your secrets and pay the price of them in suffering."

A whimper bled from my lips, a heavy kind of power building all around me which made the guards shift uncomfortably, but I still held my tongue, knowing nothing he could do would force their location from me.

"I suggest you all leave," Kalir told the guards. "For I am about to steal a slice of power from each and every deity in existence and place it into this unworthy host, and I doubt they will be happy about it once they realise what I am doing."

The guards exchanged concerned looks as the billowing power continued to build, and they all took off at once, abandoning me to this fate even as I called out after them for mercy.

"Please," I begged, looking up into the face of the only man left standing before me.

He drew closer, an iron blade in his hand which was marked with the symbol for Steelion, the god of metal, stone, and strength.

"The time for any kind of begging is long past, Esworn," Kalir said softly, closing in on me, and though I tried to recoil, that only made the iron collar cut into my flesh more deeply. "Now you shall reap the true reward of what you've done and forever pay for it with your servitude."

My heart beat faster and faster as he closed in on me, that power swelling and growing endlessly until all I could see was the fervent brightness in his eyes and before long, even that was stolen from me by the agony of the magic which he forced beneath my skin. He began to carve the symbols of the gods into my flesh, my healing affinity chasing after his blade and healing the wounds as he made them.

The gods screamed as he ripped a slice of power from each of them, forcing that magic into me with every slice of his blade, their curses striking against my ears, not one of them turning my way to offer any kind of help as their fury grew and grew.

*"The world will pay the price of what has been done here."* They hissed and spat at me, Kalir not seeming to hear them or care for their warnings as he focused on breaking me apart and remaking me in the image he had designed.

I couldn't make out their words between the agony consuming me, but I felt them, one by one I felt them cursing our kind and the way we had squandered what they'd given us. They snarled at us for twisting their rules and skirting them entirely, and they sniped at me for turning to Herdat in my time of greatest need, for taking her deal and speaking that lie.

The gods had been on the brink of forsaking us for years, and as the pitch of my screams grew louder and louder, Kalir slicing away at their magic as if doing so meant nothing at all and would come at no cost, they began to turn from us.

One by one I felt them, like splashes of acid against my skin, the burn of their rejection sinking down to my core. They were our creators, our deities, our salvation. But we had finally pushed them too far.

Agony seared through me as Kalir hissed words of magic and theft, cleaving me open and forcing the stolen essence of the gods inside me while I screamed with the agony of my immortal life being torn from me one bite at a time. But death didn't come to claim me as it should have. Instead, my magic pulsed and flared and consumed all it could as it fought to keep me breathing through every agonising second.

I lost all sense of time and space, my mind cracking apart like a lightning bolt had seared straight through me. I wasn't good or evil, I wasn't kind or cruel, I wasn't light or dark. I wasn't anything anymore. And as the roaring well of power reared up inside me, filling me so deeply that I was on the brink of losing every last scrap of myself to the essence of it, I found myself falling.

Down.

Down.

Down.

Until I hit the ground before that throne of destruction, the golden coin winking up at me as I careered towards it then fell through it, into it, tumbling impossibly further before landing on the cold, hard floor of gold at its centre.

# CHAPTER ELEVEN

My skin burned with the magic which roared inside me, a taste of every kind of power rioting in my veins and my mind spinning with the weight of it all.

*Stupid, stupid, stupid girl*, a voice hissed in the dark. My voice. And it wasn't coming from some corner of this cold and barren space, it was coming from within me. A voice which was my own and wasn't. Me and yet someone else entirely.

"Where am I?" I breathed, pushing onto my hands and knees while the magic crashed through my limbs like a tempestuous sea, and I fought to keep my balance.

I got to my feet and moved to the closest golden wall, my hand pressing to the cold metal as I looked at the gold roof above my head, the perfectly flat disc which held no doors or windows.

*Trapped. We're stuck in here because of you, stuck and alone and lost.*

I started walking, then running, my hand skimming the curved wall as I moved, hunting for a hidden door, a seam, anything at all, but the metal remained smooth and solid no matter where I searched.

I needed something to help me break out of his place, but there wasn't anything here, not so much as a speck of dust to colour the golden space surrounding me. But as my thoughts began to spiral into panic, a heavy mallet appeared in my hands out of nothing at all.

I stumbled back in shock, dropping it but then hurried to grab it again, lifting it between my hands and slamming it into the wall as hard as I could. Nothing happened. Not a dent or scratch was left behind, and the panic began to claw its way up my throat as I struck the wall repeatedly, screaming and cursing as it failed to make a mark.

As I hefted the hammer again, my mind buzzed with the echoes of memory, and I cursed myself for forgetting. I didn't care about escaping whatever this was. I only wanted the release of death now anyway.

The hammer fizzled away to nothing in my hands, a wicked dagger appearing at a single thought in its place.

"I'm coming, Aalia," I breathed, hoping my words could be heard from the Garden.

I turned the blade towards my own chest, closed my eyes and thrust the dagger straight through my heart.

Agony stole through me as I crumpled to my knees, blood spilling all around me as death came sweeping in on furious wings, and in less than a breath, I was gone, drifting, falling into the embrace of the dark…

I sucked in a sharp breath as I woke. The dagger was gone, and my flesh was unharmed where it had been punctured, the golden prison still intact around me.

"No," I gasped, pushing myself up as I hunted the dark corners of the round room for any sign of blood or the weapon, but it was all gone. As if it had never been.

*Slave to the coin,* the voice in my head mocked hatefully, and I recoiled from her words.

But before I could attempt any other form of escape from this uncertain fate, a thread tugged on the very centre of my being and the world fell away around me, the golden room disappearing before I found myself on my knees in a clearing in the woods, fat petals drifting past me on a gentle breeze.

The soft swish of fabric drew my attention to the ice-white robes on my left, and I turned to look up at Kalir with nothing but purest hatred in my eyes.

The need to destroy him rose up in me so potently that the power I had laid claim to began to glow beneath my flesh.

I made a move to stand, but before I could get my feet beneath me, he spoke.

"Kneel," he sneered, and my knees slammed into the dirt as the power of his words consumed me.

I parted my lips on some barb or curse, but whatever it had been was lost to me as a white light flared at my throat and I realised I still wore that iron collar, the thing tight to my skin and the spikes impaled deep in my flesh. I gasped as I clutched at it, fighting to get it off me even as the light flared brighter and a thin, golden chain appeared from the front of it.

My eyes widened in horror as the chain snaked away from me, slithering through the grass towards Kalir before shooting up and snapping itself tightly around his wrist. The chain yanked tight, and I cried out as a connection formed between the two of us like a bridge between our souls, his dark and twisted essence worming its way inside of me while he groaned in a show of ecstasy.

The chain faded away but the tug of it didn't diminish in the slightest, and as the corners of Kalir's mouth lifted, I felt fear unlike anything I'd experienced before.

"You are remade, Esworn," Kalir cooed. "Born into eternal power and robbed of all free will. The master of your destiny is the one who owns your coin." He lifted the golden coin before me and I lunged for it, trying to snatch it from his hand. "Stop."

His command was like the toll of a bell within me, my body jerking to a halt, my fingers brushing the edge of the coin while he smirked at me triumphantly and my heart thundered to an impossible rhythm.

"From now until the end of time, you will exist in this form. Death cannot release you. Pain cannot end you. You will be The Blessing to all who possess you, though no doubt it may seem more like a curse to you."

"Why?" I breathed, unable to take in all he was saying.

"Even I cannot lay full claim to the power of the gods. But you, what you now are, you can. You are the most powerful creature on this fair earth, and everything is possible to you, aside from free will. You will bow to the word of your master, and together, we will remake the world as I see fit."

"No." I tried to back up, shaking my head as I reached for the collar at my throat once more, fighting to rip it from my flesh while begging every god I could think of to save me from this fate. But they were gone, their backs turned on me and my kind, no lingering spark of them remaining.

Death was what I sought, a place in the Garden at my sister's side. This fate was too cruel, too wicked. I couldn't be a slave to this monster. I wouldn't.

But as Kalir parted his lips on his first command, all free will fled from me entirely, and the power which had been forced upon me rose to follow his will. Whatever demand he made of me would be done. I would forge his every wish from this tempestuous power in me and hand them to him. Blood, glory, death, destruction. If he willed it, he would have it all. This monster made into a god by the magic he could command through me. And as I gazed into his cruel eyes which held nothing but malice and greed, I knew I would soon be the maker of purest evil and all I had once been would be forgotten.

# ALSO BY
# CAROLINE PECKHAM
# &
# SUSANNE VALENTI

**A Game of Malice and Greed**

*(M/F, Fantasy Romance Series)*

A Kingdom of Gods and Ruin

A Game of Malice and Greed


**Brutal Boys of Everlake Prep**

*(Complete Reverse Harem Bully Romance Contemporary Series)*

Kings of Quarantine

Kings of Lockdown

Kings of Anarchy

Queen of Quarantine

**

**Dead Men Walking**

*(Reverse Harem Dark Romance Contemporary Series)*

The Death Club

Society of Psychos

**

**The Harlequin Crew**

*(Reverse Harem Mafia Romance Contemporary Series)*

Sinners Playground

Dead Man's Isle

Carnival Hill

Paradise Lagoon

**Harlequinn Crew Novellas**

Devil's Pass

\*\*

**Dark Empire**

*(Dark Mafia Contemporary Standalones)*

Beautiful Carnage

Beautiful Savage

\*\*

**The Ruthless Boys of the Zodiac**

*(Reverse Harem Paranormal Romance Series - Set in the world of Solaria)*

Dark Fae

Savage Fae

Vicious Fae

Broken Fae

Warrior Fae

**Zodiac Academy**

*(M/F Bully Romance Series- Set in the world of Solaria, five years after Dark Fae)*

The Awakening

Ruthless Fae

The Reckoning

Shadow Princess

Cursed Fates

Fated Thrones

Heartless Sky

Sorrow and Starlight

The Awakening - As told by the Boys

## Zodiac Academy Novellas
Origins of an Academy Bully

The Big A.S.S. Party

## Darkmore Penitentiary
*(Reverse Harem Paranormal Romance Series - Set in the world of Solaria,*
*ten years after Dark Fae)*

Caged Wolf

Alpha Wolf

Feral Wolf

**

## The Age of Vampires
*(Complete M/F Paranormal Romance/Dystopian Series)*

Eternal Reign

Eternal Shade

Eternal Curse

Eternal Vow

Eternal Night

Eternal Love

**

## Cage of Lies
*(M/F Dystopian Series)*

Rebel Rising

**

## Tainted Earth
*(M/F Dystopian Series)*

Afflicted

Altered

Adapted

Advanced

**

### The Vampire Games

*(Complete M/F Paranormal Romance Trilogy)*

V Games

V Games: Fresh From The Grave

V Games: Dead Before Dawn

*

### The Vampire Games: Season Two

*(Complete M/F Paranormal Romance Trilogy)*

Wolf Games

Wolf Games: Island of Shade

Wolf Games: Severed Fates

*

### The Vampire Games: Season Three

Hunter Trials

*

### The Vampire Games Novellas

A Game of Vampires

**

### The Rise of Issac

*(Complete YA Fantasy Series)*

Creeping Shadow

Bleeding Snow

Turning Tide

Weeping Sky

Failing Light

Made in the USA
Las Vegas, NV
03 March 2023